James H. Graff, Gertrude Fenton

Cora

The Romance of Three Years

James H. Graff, Gertrude Fenton

Cora
The Romance of Three Years

ISBN/EAN: 9783337349233

Printed in Europe, USA, Canada, Australia, Japan

Cover: Foto ©Andreas Hilbeck / pixelio.de

More available books at www.hansebooks.com

C O R A;

OR,

THE ROMANCE OF THREE YEARS.

A Novel.

BY GERTRUDE FENTON.

LONDON:

F. ENOS ARNOLD, 49, ESSEX ST., STRAND, W.C.

1869.

CONTENTS.

CORA;

OR,

THE ROMANCE OF THREE YEARS.

CHAPTER I.

CORA'S SECRET.

A NOVEMBER evening was closing gloomily in, the rain was falling in dull plashes on the pavement, and the gloom was relieved here and there by stray gas lamps, which only made the scene more dreary. It was a night to draw the curtains closer and shut out the dark outside world, and to gather comfort from within.

On this night a man beyond the prime of life was hurrying across Westminster Bridge. He was evidently, by his figure and attire, not one of the hewers of wood, or drawers of water, of this world, but his thin coat, and well-worn boots showed that Dame Fortune had not of late been kind to him. After some time he turned down one of those small streets which lie near the Victoria Theatre, and knocked at a house, the aspect of which was even more desolate than that of its dilapidated neighbours. After he had waited a few moments, the door was opened by a young girl, by whom he was evidently expected, and without a word, he passed into a room on the ground floor.

The room was miserably furnished, there was little fire in the grate, in spite of the cold and rain, but what

1

there was lit up a clever, care-worn face, with sharp, pinched features, and a look of hope deferred. As he drew near the fire a woman, pale and wasted, but with traces of great beauty, rose to meet him, and looked into his face with anxious eyes.

"Any luck to-day?" she asked.

"No," he answered, "luck and I have shaken hands long ago. I have been promised money, but—we cannot live on promises."

"Ah!" sighed the woman, "it is always so; it would be better, much better, if we were all dead."

"Hush, mother, do not say that; better times are in store. Remember, there is never a black cloud but the sun shines behind."

It was the girl who had admitted him who spoke with bright, cheery accents, and making the fire give out a faint blaze, she set a tray on the table, and began to prepare the poor evening meal.

"Let us forget our troubles to-night. Come, poor papa, let me take your wet coat. See, there, now, we shall all be better for a cup of tea."

The man regarded her with a wan smile, yet there was a look of anxious pride in his eyes, as there might well be, for she was his daughter, and one in whom a parent could not fail to rejoice. About sixteen years of age, she looked still younger; she was rather small, with a beautifully rounded figure, and aristocratic hands and feet; her head was small, and well set on a tall, white throat; the face was open and honest, and what many people would have called beautiful, and yet the features, taken separately, were far from perfect; the nose was neither Roman, Grecian, nor of any particular stamp; the mouth was large but well formed, and the teeth small and white; the eyes were very large, and of no settled colour, but black, blue, brown, and grey by turns, according to the feelings to which they gave expression; the eyebrows were by no means arched, rather the reverse, and thick, but to have altered them would have been to spoil the face. The only real and unmistakable beauty was a quantity of golden hair, which was drawn off the low, broad forehead, and knotted at the back of the head. The girl was very poorly dressed, still there was something that showed she was not born to the station in which she was now found.

This, indeed, was most true. Twenty years before Edgar Wilton, her father, was a man of good position in the mercantile world, his name quoted, and his shrewdness unequalled. Rather late in life he fell in love with a beautiful woman, of extravagant habits, but without money; they married, and for a time all went smoothly on. At length a financial crisis came, and Edgar Wilton awoke one morning a beggar, with a wife and child to support. The shock prostrated him, and he rose from his bed of sickness a prematurely old man. He found his wife settled into a querulous invalid, and the world that had seemed to him so bright in the morning and noon of life, had grown dark, shadowy, and overcast this November evening. He had now to put his shoulder to the wheel, and first he sought those whom he had befriended in wealth and asked their aid, but found their memories oblivious of the past. Having tried every resource in vain, he was on the brink of despair, but at last he obtained an opening as clerk in a merchant's office, and managed to struggle on, until, to crown his misfortunes, his sight began to fail him. He was unable to retain his situation, had since then been living on the proceeds of furniture, clothes, and the return of small sums of money lent by him in better days, when people felt either honest or amiable enough to respond to his appeals. At last all seemed to fail him. The waves of adversity were hard to breast with both tide and wind against him, and he had even lost sight of the beacon light of hope, and given himself up to the dark waters of despair.

This despair, however, was not shared by Cora; she was one of those bright natures that go on hoping against hope, and seeing a ray of light even in the darkest storm. On this evening she seemed even brighter and gayer than was her wont. The poor meal would have been eaten in silence but for her; but her cheerfulness was contagious, and her hopeful words and lively sallies lightened the father's burdened heart, and even brought a smile to the forlorn mother's lips. Yet had either marked her with deep scrutiny, they would have perceived that she was ill at ease. Her gaiety was forced, and she regarded both at times with quiet, furtive glances, as if meditating some confession which she dared not trust herself to express in words.

Suspecting nothing, and observing nothing, they only felt the comfort of her light spirits; yet in time her very cheerfulness (perhaps because assumed) seemed to jar with their sombre thoughts, and the querulous mother suddenly bade her be silent.

"This is no time for jesting," she said sharply; "to-morrow we shall not have bread to eat."

"Surely yes," returned Cora, "Heaven will not suffer us to starve."

"What misery has it not suffered us to feel—short of that?" was the retort. "Would that I could die and forget it all."

"No, no, mother," pleaded Cora, earnestly, "we shall yet be happy once more. Who knows what a day may bring forth? Who can say what even to-morrow may do for us?"

She spoke with strange earnestness, and the tears filled her eyes and choked her voice.

The ruined man, startled by her tone, turned from the fire into which he had been gazing, and looked earnestly into her face.

Under that gaze its pallor changed to crimson.

"You spoke," he said, "as if—as if you saw the clue to some way out of our miseries? Is this so? Have you——"

"Do not question me, father," she interrupted, burying her face in her hands while she spoke. "Ask me nothing—I cannot answer you."

The eyes of the husband and wife met. They were startled, and perhaps the mind of each shaped forth a thought—a fear— to which neither dared give utterance. The temptations of the poor are many, and assume shapes almost irresistible. And they were very poor.

"You have a secret from us?" said the mother, reproachfully.

"Only for to-night," was the hurried response; "to-morrow you shall know all."

"And if to-morrow, why not to-night?"

The tone was sharp and imperious. The girl trembled.

"Because—because"—she began, then faltered, then suddenly rose from her chair.

"Is it because you dare not tell us?" asked her father, sternly.

"No! Indeed, indeed, it is not, but I cannot trust myself to speak to-night of what may end in nothing. I will not incur your displeasure until there is need, or raise your hopes only to dash them to the ground. Oh, mother—father—trust me, I beseech you, and trust also in the Providence that watches over us even in the darkest hour."

With these passionate words she embraced each, and with tearful cheeks hurried from the room as if unable longer to master her feelings in their presence.

CHAPTER II.

A NEW LEAF IN LIFE.

WHAT was Cora Wilton's secret?

A very simple one, yet it haunted her sleep that night, mingling with her dreams, and wakening her to the dull realities of life, long before the dawn of the late and gloomy November morning. As soon as the light would permit she rose, and attiring herself as neatly as the state of her poor wardrobe would permit, she stole down stairs and out into the street before any one else in the house was stirring. It was not that there was any need of her being thus early abroad, but she was anxious to escape questioning, and to carry out a purpose she had in her own way.

When the fact that she was absent became known to those to whom she was so endeared, their uneasiness was great. Her words and manner over night had made a painful impression on them. They knew her to be good and true, but the young are inexperienced, and they feared lest the strong desire to improve their position should have induced her to take some rash step which she might afterwards bitterly repent.

Great, therefore, was their delight when, towards noon, she presented herself at the door, her eyes beaming, and her face radiant with satisfaction.

"Oh, Cora, what has happened?" they demanded in a breath.

"All that I had hardly dared to hope," she replied.

"Indeed! You bring good news, then?"

"I do, father, for I have secured employment, which will keep us from starvation."

"Employment for me?" he asked.

"No," was her proud answer, "for myself."

Then with eager lips and a burning cheek she told the story of her morning's adventure. Their poverty, she explained, had driven her to ask the daughter of a neighbour—Ellen Morris—how she contrived to keep herself and her family in respectability? The answer was, that she had an engagement at a theatre,—was, in fact, one of the ballet at Drury Lane, where she would appear in the forthcoming Pantomime. The girl had added, that it might be possible to find an opening there for a friend; had made enquiries, which resulted favourably, and in brief, Cora had that day been formally engaged at the great theatre, at the munificent remuneration of twelve shillings per week!

"What! you, Cora! Engaged at a theatre!" cried Mrs. Wilton, with an outburst of indignant severity, as this recital was finished. "And so, this was your secret? No wonder you feared to take us into your confidence. At a theatre, indeed!"

Poor Cora! She had not expected this. Her good fortune had inspired her with the brightest dreams. Already she fancied herself a great actress, with the world at her feet. She had pictured the triumphs she was going to achieve; how rich she was going to be, and the great Lord who, at last, was going to fall at her knees and marry her, so that the rest of her days might be passed in boundless affluence! The walk home had been like flying, so eager was she to tell the good news, the joyful surprise, never dreaming that the slightest objection could be made to it. But we all have our disap-pointments in this life, and poor Cora's was not a slight one when she saw the displeasure of her parents at the step she had taken.

All her bright dreams vanished.

For a time those who loved her too well to expose her to avoidable temptation, would not hear of it. They had all the customary prejudices against the stage, and espe-cially against the ballet. But real want is a good advo-cate, and when it was urged by Cora that the engage-ment was made, that there was actually money within their reach, while, as opposed to this, there was nothing but the blankest poverty, and most absolute starvation, they yielded : assented, and reluctantly suffered her to carry out the plan she had formed.

So Cora turned the new leaf in her life, and entered upon her arduous duties. The long and tedious rehear-sals soon dispelled the illusions she had indulged in, but when the Pantomime was really produced, and was a success, and especially when, through the illness of one of the coryphées, she was promoted and enrolled as one of the regular ballet, at a pound a-week, all her enthu-siasm returned, and she felt supremely happy. The satisfaction she felt was increased by her popularity in the theatre. She gained many friends among her com-panions by her light and laughing nature, while her self-denial and gentleness caused those who would have been jealous, to respect her.

And were these people to whose respect she ought to have been indifferent ? Surely not. They had warm hearts and generous impulses. They could practise the greatest of the Christian virtues, too, as one incident in the life of the theatre will serve to illustrate.

When Cora had been in the theatre about a month, one of the ballet—Ella Graham, by name—had the misfortune to slip on the stage, and sprained her ankle most severely. "She would be unable," the doctor said, "to dance for at least six or seven weeks." At this news the poor girl began crying bitterly; Cora's heart was touched, and taking the girl's hand in hers, she tried to comfort her, bidding her hope as perhaps the sprain would be well a great deal sooner, and the pain would not be half so severe in a day or so. Ella turned her large black eyes up into the face of her comforter, with a piteous look,—"It is not the pain that grieves me," she said, "it is losing my employment. Ah! what shall I do for my dear mother, and Eunice? They will have nothing to eat if I cannot dance." The words sunk into Cora's heart, and the group of girls round, frivolous, vain, and wild, as many of them were, felt their woman's nature touched by that wail of misery, and each determined that the mother and little sister should not want.

They had good hearts, these poor girls, under all the hard coating their struggle with the world had caused, and knew how to appreciate true devotion. We look upon them as a kind of machinery, thinking much the same as we think of the scenery, yet did we follow them to their homes, many a devoted daughter, and tender sister, should we find among them. "Ah," but then, "I hear my reader say, "I always thought ballet girls were very bad, and had carriages and grand houses, and were altogether a class of people not to be thought about!" So some of them are, but before you condemn, remember the temptations and poverty of these poor girls, and bear with and pity them.

"Dry up your tears, Ella," said a girl called Rose. "Never say die. We won't let your mother and little Eunice want; it will be hard indeed if between us we cannot make up your salary every week. What do you say, girls?"

"Yes, yes," cried nearly all the girls at once.

"I'm sure I can give a shilling a-week," said one.

"I two," said a rather gaudily dressed girl.

"Yes, you can," said Rose; "I can't give more than one; but I will give that."

"And I, and I, and I," was echoed from twenty voices. Poor Cora and a girl named Gillian were alone silent.

"I," said Cora, "can give nothing; but Ella I know will not love me the less on that account, because I love her, and feel true sympathy for her, but I too have dear ones at home to help; they would go without if I were to give," and taking Ella's hand in hers she looked into her face with loving, kindly eyes.

Ella pressed her hand, and, turning to the group of girls, said, "Thanks, thanks, I shall never forget your goodness, but I cannot take your money."

"Don't be silly," said Rose, "we will not give more than we can afford; besides, if I wanted it, I should not be too proud to take it, and supposing you could do without it, what's to become of your mother and sister?"

"Enough," said Ella, "I will accept of your kindness for a week, but only as a loan."

"All right, pay us back when you are a rich woman, that'll do."

"Ballet called," cried the call-boy; and each one rushed to her dressing-place to smooth her hair, or renew the roses on her cheeks, and then rushed down to the stage to take her respective place for the opening scene.

Incidents like these revealed to Cora the true nature of the despised ballet girl.

A month or more had passed when, one night, as Cora came up to the dressing-room, after the performances, she was astonished to find a beautiful bouquet of flowers on the dressing-place. Calling the dresser, she enquired who had left them there, and if they were for her?

"Oh! yes, miss," was the reply, "they are meant for you, fast enough; the gentleman who gave them to Cliff, the doorkeeper, said they was to be given to Miss Cora Wilton; I knew it would not be long before some of these swells fell in love with you."

"Perhaps there is a card in it," said Rose. "Let us see," and taking the flowers in her hand, she began un-

doing the paper, and out fell a card. "Yes, here it is,
see, Sir Reginald Clayton! I don't know him; who is
he? Do any of you girls know?"

"I have seen him once," said Kate, "he is tall, dark,
and very rich, I believe; whoever would have thought of
his being smitten with Cora?"

"What am I to do with the flowers?" said Cora;
"perhaps I had better leave them with Cliff to return."

"Don't be a muff," said Kate. "Keep them. The
idea of returning a bouquet!"

Poor Cora was sadly puzzled, but decided at last to
keep them. Dressing quickly, she and Ellen Morris left
the room, and prepared to walk home together. When in
the hall they met a tall, dark man, who, removing his
hat, said, "I think I have the pleasure of speaking to
Miss Wilton?"

Little Cora's heart beat fast, for she had the flowers in
her hand, and this no doubt was the donor.

"That is my name," said Cora, in a trembling voice.

"Will you allow me to accompany you? it is hardly
the thing for such pretty girls to walk home unprotected."

"We require no protection," said Ellen; "and never
allow gentlemen to walk with us. Come along, Cora."

"Pardon me," said the gentleman; "I had no idea of
being rude. Good evening, ladies."

He bowed and went. The girls walked on a few moments in silence. At last Cora said, "Ellen, how could
you be so cross to that nice gentleman. I am sure it was
very kind of him to offer to see us home, and after
sending me flowers, and all, what ill-natured girls he
will think us."

"Let him think that if he likes," said Ellen, "we are not
going to let him walk with us indeed! How silly you
are, Cora; one would think that you wished to get talked
about, like Kate, and some of the other girls; I am sure
your mamma would be very angry if she thought you
wished such a thing."

"I don't, Ellen, how can you say such a thing. You
are very unkind to me, and I am sure I have done
nothing," said poor Cora, ready to cry.

"You should not have taken the bouquet; I know it will cause some mischief yet," was Ellen's return.

By this time they reached Cora's home.

"Good night," said Ellen; "I hope you will tell your mother all about the flowers, and see what she will say."

"Oh, good-night," said Cora, in a cold, constrained voice, for she felt very angry with her friend, and although in her heart she thought her right, still Ellen had wounded her feelings.

"See, mamma," said Cora, on entering the house, "what a beautiful bouquet I had sent me." But she said nothing about the card!

Cora slept little that night.

"What a pretty name Reginald is," she said to herself. "I wonder if I shall see him again. I am sure he was very nice and kind. Whatever did Ellen mean by being so cross? No doubt he has fallen in love with me, and will ask papa to let me marry him, and then I shall have mamma and papa to live with me, and we shall be very happy."

Alas! poor Cora!

CHAPTER III.

THE CLAYTONS OF CLAYTON TOWERS.

THE Claytons of Clayton were an old and proud family, dating in origin far back into the Middle Ages. Many a noble knight had it given to the wars, and many a beautiful dame to grace the court. They had always been renowned for their valour and beauty, and not less for their wickedness.

Clayton Towers was a grand, massive old building, partly built in the reign of Edward the Fourth; but the greater part dated no further back than the time of the tyrant Henry the Eighth. The Claytons had been an unfortunate family, the result, so said an old legend, of a certain curse, which could never be removed. However that might be, certain it is that not one Clayton since that curse was pronounced had died a natural death.

The curse, so ran the legend, was brought upon them by the wickedness of a Sir Reginald Clayton, who lived in the time of James the First. He, like the rest of his family, was a remarkably handsome man; and when about twenty, fell in love with a beautiful girl, the daughter of one of his retainers. It was the old, old story of woman's devotion and credulity, and man's falsehood and baseness. For a time the girl was happy, but she found too soon that she had given her heart to one who knew not the meaning of true love, and that the heart she fondly thought her own was hers no longer. The poor girl pined and pined, shut up in the old keep at the Towers, and several months passed away in dreary solitude, for he to whom she had given all was away at court. At last a baby was born to cheer her breaking heart, and although a child of shame she loved it truly, and determined to live for its sake. Months lengthened into years, and still the recreant lover never came; at length the news was spread that Sir Reginald was going to be married to a rich lady at the court, and there began to be preparations made at the Towers for their reception. One night Sir Reginald arrived alone, and went to the old keep, to have an interview with Marion. What passed was never known, but from that night poor Marion and her child disappeared.

In due time Sir Reginald and his wife came to live at the Towers, and Marion was forgotten. Years passed, and an heir was born, and great were the feastings and rejoicings, but somehow a cloud seemed to hang over Sir Reginald. He who used to be so gay and lighthearted was seldom seen to smile. One day, when the heir was twelve years old, he was playing in the old keep, which had not been used since Marion's disappearance, and chancing to touch a knob communicating with a spring by the fireplace, the panel gave way. The boy's curiosity was roused, and, seeing a small staircase, he began descending it, but after a few steps it ended, and he saw nothing but a blank wall. This, of course, puzzled him, and he determined to question his father about it. When Sir Reginald returned from his ride, the boy related his discovery. At the mention of the panel, his father grew deadly pale, and then flew into a fearful passion, and forbade him on pain of his everlasting displeasure ever to speak of it again. The next day the door of the old keep was closed.

Years passed, and when the boy had almost grown to man's estate, his father was one day hunting in the forest near the Towers, when his horse took fright, and bolting wildly over a precipice, both horse and rider were dashed to atoms. No one mourned much for Sir Reginald; his gloomy, silent manner created more fear than love in those around him, and his son was now Sir Walter. He was a quiet, gentle youth, endowed with the beauty of his family, but up to the present time without its vices. After the year of mourning he married his cousin, and for some years all went on happily.

At last Sir Walter resolved to solve the mystery of the old keep, and one day went by himself into the room where he remembered having found the spring. On reaching the bottom of the steps he sounded the wall, and discovered, after a great deal of searching, a small door, so artfully concealed that for a time his efforts to effect an entrance were futile. At length the door gave way, and he found himself in a small room illumined only by the lamp he carried. The apartment was furnished as a bed-room, and in times gone by had no doubt been built as a hiding-place. He approached the bed, and there, to his horror, saw the skeletons of a woman and child. By them was a scroll of writing, which he secured, and closing the door on that fearful room, he retraced his steps with it in his hand, determined to read it before he proclaimed the discovery.

On reaching the library Sir Walter opened the packet, and there read the following words: " I, Marion Elmore, now dying with my son of starvation, by the inhuman cruelty of Sir Reginald Clayton, do curse him and his heirs with my last breath. May one and all die by violence until their hated name shall cease to exist. When the last of the line is dead, then only shall I rest in peace. Accursed for ever be their name!"

Here the writing became indistinct, and Sir Walter dropped the scroll, and burying his face in his hands, could scarcely realise the terror of that curse and his father's wickedness. Now, indeed, the mystery of Marion's and her son's disappearance, of which he had heard the servants speak, was explained. They had been shut up by his father and starved to death; no wonder Sir Reginald was gloomy with that fearful crime hanging over him. No doubt the dreadful curse rang in his ears day and night, and tortured him in his dying moment.

That curse! they were a doomed race! The curse had already taken effect. How awful had been his father's death! and his end, probably, would perhaps be as terrible. And his infant son, would he share the same dread fate?

The thought was maddening. What could he do to avert the destruction of his family? Nothing: he was powerless. The curse would cling to them, striking the innocent with the guilty throughout all time. From that day Sir Walter was a changed man; he became restless, and joined in the troubles already convulsing his country. He fought for his sovereign, and fell, so the curse was fulfilled in the second generation, and so it had gone on.

The Claytons had always been restless and unhappy, branded with the mark of the first murderer, and no one of them had met a natural end. Many a sad tragedy had occurred to them, and people grew almost to fear a race so evidently doomed.

The old name was almost extinct; there only remained the present Sir Reginald and his sister Maud. The male descendant of this fatal line bade fair to emulate his ancestors in their extravagance and profligacy; he inherited alike their beauty and their blackness of heart; his elegance and polish were the fair coverings to his demon soul, and this was the man who had cast his evil eye on poor little Cora. Maud Clayton was the exact opposite to her brother; he had all the dark flashing beauty of the Claytons; she, the soft loveliness of her gentle mother; he had all their vices, she all their virtues. If ever an

THE CLAYTONS OF CLAYTON TOWERS.

angel walked on earth it was sweet Maud Clayton. She
was seven years younger than her brother, a young
maiden of sweet eighteen.

See what a pretty picture she makes standing on the
steps of that old time-worn mansion! The sun is shining
on her soft brown tresses, and turning them into molten
gold, and the lovely hazel eyes are cast down; thy dream
must be a pleasant one, sweet Maud, for the cherub
mouth is wreathed in smiles. Dream on, dear Maud;
surely no curse can ever cling to one so bright, so beautiful, and good. Sin and shame can never rest on that
clear brow; no, you are the one pure lily in that great
garden of noisome weeds; they may cling round, but
they cannot stain; you rise so far above them, in your
innocence a tower of strength. Could the gentle mother who loved you so tenderly see you now, she would
indeed rejoice that the Giver of all good had bestowed
on her such a child. Perhaps even now her tender love
is shielding you, and keeping you from harm.

Maud is alone, her brother being in London. It is
seldom he honours the Towers with his presence, it is
too gloomy for him, unless, indeed, when he brings
down a company of choice companions to help him dispel
the dreariness. Maud is not yet out in the fashionable
world, but in a few months she is to make her first appearance under the auspices of a relation of her mother's, Lady Wilson. Ah, Maud! you little think how
you will sigh for the old quiet. The world that you so
long to enter is bright and beautiful to the eye as the
apples of the Dead Sea, but like them full of ashes.

"Ah, Hero, come here, you naughty old fellow," said
Maud, to a large Newfoundland dog who was basking on
the steps in a ray of sunshine, "and if you are good I
will tell you such news. Uncle Walter is coming home;
we both love Uncle Walter, don't we, Hero?"

The intelligent animal rose at the name with a look
of almost human understanding, and trotted to his fair
mistress to be caressed.

"Come Hero, let us go for our walk," and Maud
tripped down the steps, and taking a short path across

the park, entered the mead that bounded it, followed by
her faithful companion, who seemed to feel the responsi-
bility he enjoyed in protecting so fair a mistress.

Although very early spring, the trees were putting
forth their young leaves, and the sweet-scented violet
perfumed the air. It was one of those beautiful balmy
days we sometimes get in spring time, very seldom, it is
true, but that only makes them the more delightful. The
fashion now is to run down the climate of England, and
certainly, as a rule, deservedly, but when we do have a
fine day, it is, indeed, delicious. The air is pure and
fresh, the country looking so peaceful and happy, and
the birds singing as they sing nowhere else, make up
altogether a feeling of quiet enjoyment never experienced
in any other country.

After walking about half a mile through the mead
Maud came to a little cottage, hidden by the surround-
ing trees, until you were quite upon it. She was evidently a welcome and frequent visitor, for on lifting the
latch and entering, a little voice said with accents of
glee, "See, mother, here is Miss Maud." The interior
of the cottage was a perfect picture of neatness and
cleanliness.

"How is Charlie to-day?" said Maud, crossing the
room to a sofa on which lay a little wasted boy; "the
day is so fine that I thought I would bring Hero to see
him."

The mother, a fair, comely-looking woman, who was
sitting at needlework, rose, and placing a chair for her
visitor near the sofa, said—

"Not quite so well to-day, miss; he was very bad in
the night, but the sight of you always makes him better.
God bless you for your kindness in coming."

"Kindness, indeed," said Maud; "why, Charlie and
I are the greatest friends, and when he gets stronger,
and the warm weather arrives, he is coming to see me."

Alas! one look in the little face was sufficient reply.
It was but too obvious that the angel soul would soon
desert the frail little frame, and Charlie would be one
more bright spirit in the heavenly choir.

"See, here are some violets," said Maud, after stooping down and kissing the little face, and placing the flowers on his pillow; "don't they smell sweetly, darling?"

The child did not reply, but took Maud's hand in his little wasted ones with a look of intense satisfaction.

"I'm going to stay with Charlie all the afternoon if you please, Mrs. Morgan," said Maud.

Charlie uttered a cry of delight.

"Will you sing to me?"

"Yes," said Maud; "what shall I sing to you, Charlie?"

"All about the dear angels."

"Very well, darling."

And in a sweet low voice she began—

"Dear angel, ever at my side,
How loving thou must be,
To leave thy home in heaven,
To guard a wretch like me."

"There's an angel now with me, isn't there?" said Charlie; "he always stays with me, doesn't he? so I'm never afraid now when I'm in the dark, because I know he is there, and he won't let anything hurt me, will he?"

"No, Charlie, he is sent to take care of you, and loves you all so much more, much more, even, than I do."

"And he's very beautiful, isn't he?"

"Yes."

"And when I die he will take me up to heaven, and then my back won't be bad, will it?"

"No, darling, you will be a little bright angel with wings."

"And shall I see you?"

"If I am good enough, dear."

"Oh, I wish we could go now, and father and mother too. How happy we should be, and I should see the dear angel, and thank him for taking care of me," said Charlie.

"Try and go to sleep, darling, and when you wake up

2

I will tell you a pretty story," said Maud, noticing that the little eager face was flushed and feverish.

"I'll try," said Charlie, and holding Maud's hand, he was soon sleeping.

In about an hour Charlie awoke refreshed, and Maud fulfilled her promise, and story after story was poured into the eager little listener's ears. At last she rose to go.

"My darling," she said, "it is getting late—almost four, so good-bye."

"Will you come again to-morrow?" said Charlie.

"Perhaps; but the day after, for certain."

After kissing her little favourite and bidding Mrs. Morgan send up to the Towers for anything that the child wanted, Maud bent her steps homewards. Her approach was perceived by her old governess, Miss Meadowes, who came out to meet her.

"I began to be quite uneasy about you," she said, as Maud entered the hall followed by her four-footed companion. "It is getting quite dusk."

"Oh, there is no fear, dear, with Hero; he always takes care of me, don't you?" said Maud, stooping to caress her pet.

"Yes; but my darling, it is getting damp, and if you should take cold your cough would come on, and then whatever would your Uncle Walter say to my not taking better care of you?"

"Dear Uncle Walter," said Maud, "I'm sure I shall love him—oh, so much!"

Mr. Walter Earl was the brother of Maud's mother, and ever since her death had resided abroad. Maud scarcely remembered him, but his letters to her were full of love and tenderness, and the stories Miss Meadowes had told her of his devotion to his dead sister, her mother, had quite won her heart, and she looked forward to his return with delight. What plans she had made! And now her dream was going to be realised, and Uncle Walter, after an absence of fifteen years, was coming home, was even now on his way, and might arrive at any moment.

"Do you think uncle will come to-night?" said Maud. "He could get here by this time, could he not?"

"Yes, dear, if he travelled straight through; if so, he will be here in a few moments, because the express was due at Eldon Station at half-past three, and now it is nearly five, and it does not take more than an hour and a quarter to drive from Eldon here; but go, my dear, and change your dress. I am sure your feet are wet coming across that damp grass."

Maud obeyed.

"I wonder," she said to herself, as she went to her room, "if Uncle Walter will come to-night, I do so hope he will. Surely I hear the sound of wheels. I must make haste, for if it should be he, and I not at the door to welcome him, I should never forgive myself."

In a few moments Maud had made the desired changes in her dress, and was in the hall, as a postchaise drove up to the door, and a gentleman alighted.

"You are Uncle Walter, I am sure," said Maud, bounding down the steps, and seizing his hand. "Welcome, welcome, home."

The gentleman gazed into the eager, upturned face, and bending down, kissed the pure white forehead.

"You are my niece Maud; I should have known you anywhere from your likeness to your mother."

Mr. Earl was a tall man of some forty-three or four years of age, but looked older; he was not handsome, yet few women, looking in Walter Earl's face, would say he was plain; the features, in themselves, were commonplace enough, but the eyes were clear, frank, and loving, and when he smiled, his face was transformed, and became almost beautiful, such wonderful fascination was there in it. As he stood now in that old room, with his eyes full of tenderness, fixed on the daughter of his dead sister, no wonder Maud thought him handsomer than any one she had ever seen. Love is, indeed, a beautifier, and effects such changes that even ugly faces are made beautiful by its magic power.

"Dear, dear uncle, I have so longed to see you; and you will love me, because you say I am like mamma.

Oh, how happy I am !" said Maud, almost ready to cry
for joy. "You must stay always with us now, and
never go away again. Where is Hero?—he knows you
already, I have talked to him so much about you. I
will go and find him."

"Stay, dear," said Miss Meadowes, "remember your
uncle has been travelling; he is, no doubt, tired, and re-
quires some refreshment."

"What a thoughtless girl I am! of course he does!
Poor uncle, come into the dining-room. Dinner is all
ready, I know, because we expected you, and Miss Meadowes said I might dine late to stay with you if you
came," said Maud, "and after dinner you shall be introduced to Hero."

What a happy meal that was! Maud overflowing
with happiness, telling her uncle all the news of her little
world, as though she had known him all her life, and he
enjoying the love and attention, so new to the lonely
man, who had been so long an exile; her fresh young
voice carried him back to the days of his youth, when his
sister and he were all the world to each other. It was,
indeed, a pleasure to come back after long years of absence, and find such love and rest. He had scarcely
dared to hope that a Clayton, even though the child of
his dead sister, could ever be like this, but Maud was the
true daughter of his dearly loved sister in every way.

And as he looked upon her—he with his knowledge of
the dark cloud which hung over the race of the Claytons
—a silent prayer to Heaven rose from the depths of his
loving heart, a prayer that her purity and goodness might
save her from the inevitable doom. It was a happy, happy
night. They sat together, the returned wanderer and
the girl who knew so little of the world he had mas-
tered; they talked of that dead sister to whom Maud
owed her existence, of his wanderings and adventures,
and so rapidly did the hours pass that it was as if they
had been startled from a brief but happy dream when the
Towers clock tolled forth the hour of midnight.

Both rose at the sound, and a shudder passed over the

fair girl's sensitive frame, as if she listened to the knell of her life's happiness. Was that feeling in any sense prophetic?

CHAPTER IV

ON THE BRINK.

THE Pantomime was at its last gasp. One more week, and it would be over. Fairies and elves would then troop down to the country theatres, there to hide themselves, until the following Christmas shall call them back to life. Poor Cora! It was now a month since we last saw her, and, seemingly, time had not brought happiness with it; her step was less full of buoyancy, and her eyes looked red with tears. She is young for such sighs of sorrow. Only a month ago we left her a little bright-eyed maiden. Surely so short a time cannot have wrought a change so great? Unhappily it was the case. Cora was not happy; her first deception necessitated others, and that of itself to a frank nature is torture, so true is it that to stray from the path of virtue is very, very easy, but to regain it an almost Herculean task.

Cora had seen Sir Reginald several times since that memorable night, and although nothing could be more courteous and deferential than his manner (for he was too accomplished in his arts to frighten before he had fairly entrapped the bird), still Cora felt she was doing wrong in seeing him at all without her mother's sanction, and she had no one to advise her; for Ellen Morris was cross and would not speak to her, and Ella was still unable to attend the theatre. Poor little silly Cora! you are like one on the brink of a precipice.

One evening Cora was in the dressing-room; the performance was nearly over; she had ten minutes before she went on for the last scene. No one was in the room with her but the girl called Kate.

"What a love of a ring! Diamonds and opals, I declare! Why don't you put it on?" said Kate, taking a small box containing a ring of some value out of Cora's hands.

"Because I am not going to keep it," said Cora. "It came just now, and I shall return it to-night."

"What for?"

"Why, I could not keep it; my mother would be dreadfully cross with me. Besides it is not right to take rings from gentlemen," said Cora.

"What a simpleton you are; there is no more harm in taking rings than taking flowers, and you need never tell your mother anything about it. I only wish some one would send me rings; you would see how soon I'd take them!"

"How very pretty it is," said Cora, "and the first ring I ever had; but it is no use, I must return it."

So she replaced it in the box with a sigh, and went down to the stage.

That night, as she left, Sir Reginald Clayton was waiting for Cora outside the theatre, and seemed not at all surprised when she put the box containing the ring into his hand, saying in a trembling voice, "Indeed, I am very much obliged, but I cannot take it. I never had a ring in all my life, and mamma would be very angry with me."

Poor Cora could say no more, and fairly broke down, in her excuses.

"Forgive me, my dear Miss Wilton; you are quite right. I was very wrong to offer it, but I saw it in a shop window to-day, and could not resist the temptation of buying it, thinking how pretty it would look on your hand. But it is not of the slightest consequence," he added, in an injured tone of voice.

"He is vexed with me now," thought Cora. "Oh! if I only had some one to advise me what to do."

Not another word was spoken, and on reaching the other side of the bridge Sir Reginald bade her a cold "Good night," and retraced his steps.

"I shall never see him again," said Cora to herself, as she hurried along. "Perhaps I ought to have taken the ring; but it is too late now. Oh! how unhappy I am!"

It was soon the last night of the Pantomime, and Coras heart beat fast with anxiety. She feared to see Sir

Reginald, and yet the thought of never beholding him again was torture to the poor girl. The first piece is over, and the overture to the Pantomime had commenced. The opening scene was a fairy dell, and Cora was discovered, surrounded by others of the *corps de ballet*. When she summoned courage to look at the audience, her eyes encountered those of Sir Reginald, fixed upon her. Poor Cora! All the good resolutions she had made vanished before that glance. Cora was in a dream all through the performance; she thought it would never end; but at last, to her intense relief, the curtain fell. How quickly she dressed and was out of the theatre! On leaving she saw with a sense of relief that Sir Reginald was there, though she had almost feared he would not be, and his manner was sweet and gentle. "I thought never to see you again, Cora" (it was the first time he had ever called her by her christian name, and the sound sent a thrill through her heart; she never thought her name so pretty before), "but I could not banish you from my mind. Cora, I love you! I cannot exist without you. I have been wild, careless, dissipated if you will, but never until now have I felt love's magic power. You are my sole thought; life without you has no charms for me." Much more in this strain did Sir Reginald say to win the simple child to her destruction, and at last he prevailed upon her to accept the ring she had refused. Moreover, when they parted, he had succeeded so far as to exact a promise from Cora that she would meet him clandestinely the next evening, another step taken in the path of deceit, which leads to misery and death. What Cora's feelings were that night when she received her mother's kiss of affection and trust may be imagined; but she was too far on the road to turn back for a mother's kiss; it would take something harder and sterner than that. The hand of him she loved could alone tear the veil from her eyes and expose his baseness, to her sorrow.

After parting with Cora, Sir Reginald gave a sigh of relief, and lighting a cigar, strolled back in the direction of Pall Mall. Could Cora have seen the evil expression on the countenance of him she thought so good and true, her delusion would have been dispelled. "What a little prude it is," said Sir Reginald to himself, "and yet those eyes are worth the trouble. I think the girl loves me, although either too shy or too well schooled to say so; still the meeting to-morrow is a great step. What a pretty creature it is! I really believe I am half in love myself. The fellows at the Club will envy me my good fortune. What a pity she is not a lady, and then one could marry her and settle down a respectable member of society, as Merton calls it; but as she is only a ballet girl the thing is perfectly impossible. Some fellows have been fools enough to do such a thing, but a Clayton? Never! Besides it would be dull work after the honeymoon was over. No, no my fair Cora; you must be mine, but on far easier terms. And, after all, she will be much better off with me than in that theatre. How they manage to live I don't know, on a pound a week, and they don't any of them get much more I know. She will, no doubt, be in a state of fear and remorse at first, but that will soon wear off when she gets accustomed to it, and fine dresses and rich jewelry will soon reconcile her; for I really like the girl, and mean to be generous to her."

With these charming resolutions and plans, Sir Reginald arrived at his Club. All the next day Cora was in alternate states of hope and fear. When night came she sallied forth to meet Sir Reginald, on pretence of paying a visit to a friend. Ah! poor mother, how fearful would have been your anxiety had you known that instead of the innocent converse with a girlish friend, your cherished child was listening to the voice of the deceiver. She who two months ago was your truthful merry child, is so no longer; the whirlwind of passion has swept over her soul, changing her very nature, and taking away for ever the careless gaiety of youth.

Cora was late at the rendezvous, and Sir Reginald began to fear lest she should after all draw back from her promise, and had almost decided to return, when she appeared.

"You are late, darling," he said, "but now you are here we will not waste the time in reproaches. You know

I love you; be mine and we will never part. Think of the happiness in store for us. Say, do you love me? If so, consent to my suit."

This was so exactly what Cora in her airy castles had planned, that the great lord who was going to marry her would say, that she was quite sure he meant all he said, and looking in his face with her truthful eyes, said, "If papa will let me marry you, I shall be so glad. Because I do love you very much," she added, with a blush.

This was not the answer Sir Reginald expected, and for a few moments he was taken aback at the innocence of the girl he was striving to bring to shame and ruin; but his evil genius did not desert him for long, and he poured such a flood of eloquence into poor Cora's ears, that before the interview closed he had impressed her with the idea that he was the most disinterested of human creatures, and only wanted a fitting opportunity to gain her parents' consent, but that in the meantime it was absolutely necessary that she should be perfectly silent.

"It is only for a time, dear child," he said, "but circumstances over which I have no control compel me to ask this of you. You would not, I know, harm me for the world, but one word at present might bring ruin."

What the nature of that ruin was he did not say, but Cora believed him implicitly, and determined to suffer anything rather than betray him by a single word, although her heart was brimming over with happiness, which she longed to tell her mother. Alas! Could she have known the baseness of his designs her heart would have broken with sorrow.

"The task is harder than I thought," said Sir Reginald to himself, as he sat over his breakfast next morning, "but it can only be a question of time, for she loves me dearly; but that was a poser when she consented to marry me on condition her father approved of me. Indeed! as though she had been a duchess! But I like her all the better; the chase is far more exciting. That was a piece of real innocence: no acting there. Wherever can she have passed her life? But, to be sure, at sixteen one ought to find that sort of thing, although it is a rarity.

The child's trustfulness almost makes me determine to give her up, and go down and see Maud; but then the fellows will laugh at me so. No, I must go on with it now. It is too late to recede. Besides, the girl loves me, and she would suffer more by that, and, after all, what will she lose? She holds no position in the world, and although her parents will, no doubt, rave and all that sort of thing, at first, when they see her happy and able to give them more money than she now does, they will come round."

Not one thought of the pure soul that is to be sacrificed!

"One o'clock, I declare," said Sir Reginald; "and I promised to meet Gifford at half-past at Tattersall's about that horse. Here, Adolphe!" calling to his valet, "where are my coat, hat, boots? Confound that fellow, he is never about when he's wanted, and I would not miss seeing Gifford for a cool thousand. Oh, you are there, are you," continued Sir Reginald, addressing a rather sinister-looking Frenchman, who appeared to answer to his master's impatient call. "Why the devil don't you come at once when I ring, and not keep me waiting all day."

The man made no answer, but could Sir Reginald have seen the look of diabolical hate on his servant's features when he passed into his dressing-room he would perhaps have paused to consider the advisability of trusting him. "Like master like man," is an old saying, and a true one. Very few bad masters have good servants, and Sir Reginald was not an exception to the rule. He had taken the man into his service some years before, when on the Continent, and many a dark page in his master's life had been unfolded to Adolphe. This man was by nature unscrupulous, crafty, and unforgiving, and a circumstance that had long ago escaped Sir Reginald's memory, had made the man his bitter enemy —an enemy who only waited his opportunity to wreak his vengeance on his trusting employer.

But of this Sir Reginald was wholly unsuspicious, as he rode out with his customary jaunty air and a smile on his handsome face.

During the very time Sir Reginald was hurrying to meet his friend at Tattersall's, Cora was wending her way towards the centre of theatrical life in all its numerous phases, Bow Street. There you may meet Richard the Third in shabby clothes, and find your Desdemona, a very common-place looking person after all. But shabby or grand, poor or rich, struggling on, or at the top of the tree, the members of the sock and buskin can never be mistaken, and to their honour be it said, that whatever their failings, hardness of heart is not among them. They move in a minor world of their own, where jealousy and envy have their sway ; but who, if distress overtake one of their little band, comes forth so nobly to assist as the poor actor ? They are like children in their feelings, and heroes in their triumphs. We hear of their faults, but their virtues are seldom known, except to God, who sees in secret, but will reward openly

Cora was going to one of the numerous theatrical agents, to put her name down for an engagement, Drury Lane being closed, and she consequently out of employment.

"What do you want, Miss ?" said the agent to Cora. "Here is a second walking lady wanted, at the Theatre Royal, Middleton ?"

"But," said Cora, "I have never acted before."

"Well, that is certainly a drawback, but here is a thing will suit you exactly, a lady wanted for respectable utility at the Theatre Royal, Elmerton, must be young and attractive ; salary one pound one shilling a week."

"Any thing for me to-day, Mr. Morton ?" interrupted a voice, and Cora, turning round, saw a rather strangely dressed person, about thirty, with the traces of beauty, but so pinched and worn-looking, that she was pitiful to behold.

"No, Miss Green, but if you come to-morrow, at two, I will see."

"That is what you have said every day for two weeks past," rejoined the woman, with a sigh, as she left the room.

"Sit down, Miss ?" said the agent to Cora. " I expect

the manager of the Theatre Royal, Elmerton, at two, and then he can see you, and make arrangements."

Cora sat down in a corner, and had an opportunity of learning much of the life she was about to enter.

"Well, old fellow, how are you?" said a tall man, with his hat placed rakishly on one side, and a pair of carefully mended gloves on; "anything in my way to-day?"

"Sit down, I expect several managers this morning, and may hear of something to suit you. Ah, Johnny! you are the very man I want," cried the agent, jumping up, and seizing a stout, fat man, in a plaid suit of bright colours.

"All right, my friend, what wantest thou with me?" said the man called Johnny, putting himself in an extravagantly comic attitude. A whispered conversation ensued, which ended in their both retiring to the nearest public-house, to talk the matter over and have a glass together.

During the agent's absence many people entered, and by the time he returned, the outer room, in which Cora sat, was quite full. What a singular scene it was! The room devoid of furniture, save a number of chairs and an old ricketty table, but the walls covered with theatrical announcements and bills. Here might be read that the greatest living wonder, Miss Adelina de Montgomery, would astonish the public by her unrivalled performance in the "Murderer's Mother," or the "Blood-red Stain," in which piece she took six characters, and sang a song. Then again one saw the startling announcement that Mr. Henri Ethelbert would die every night, until further notice, at the Theatre Royal, Black Lock, and many other equally astounding notices. Cora read these marvels with interest, and wondered if any of the people she saw were Mr. Henri Ethelbert or Miss Adelina; and well she might, for a stranger set of people were never congregated together. In one corner two men were fencing with their walking-sticks, to the imminent danger of a quiet-looking old gentleman who sat near them, placidly looking on. There again was a tall, thin man, detailing his grievance to a round, fat one, with goggle eyes; and

a young, good-looking fellow, was saying to his particular
friend and crony, "Die, villain, die!" as he playfully
poked him in the ribs with his walking-stick. Here were
the heavy men, comedians, walking gentlemen, leading
men, and comic Irishmen. Then as to ladies, all walks
were represented. There sat Emilia De Lancey, called
in the bills some years before, "the enchantress" who
played Lady Macbeth like an angel; and by her side sat
Miss Marion Johaness, a laughing, merry girl, who was
her particular friend. These two were inseparable, and
never took an engagement apart; they always went as
leading lady and chambermaid. Then again there were
two pretty-looking girls, much better and more quietly
dressed than their neighbours, known as duet singers,
and very much in request, to judge by the rather cold
reception the older ladies gave them, and the stage
whisper in which Miss De Lancey indulged to a friend
—"There are those two Miss Merediths just come in; I
can't endure them, they give themselves such airs. And
as to singing, my dear, I never heard such screaming in
all my life."

At length the agent returned in a great bustle, and
apologising to some for his absence, pleading business,
"which you know must be attended to. Ah! my
dear," said he to Miss Emilia, "when did you come to
town? Just step into my room; I have something to
say to you, and you too, my dear," to Miss Marion,—
"together as usual. I see you will never get married at
that rate, because no one but a Mormon can marry you
both."

And with a laugh at his wit, he led the way into his
little sanctum, followed by Miss Emilia and her friend.
Poor Cora was wondering how much longer she should
have to wait, when a sudden hush and look of eager
expectance proclaimed the arrival of some one of importance, and the Manager of the Theatre Royal, Middleton,
entered. He was a stout, good tempered looking man,
with a rather pompous air, and after giving a managerial
nod to those with whom he was acquainted, he went into
the agent's private room. In a few moments Miss

Emilia and her friend reappeared, and bowing to their acquaintances, left.

"Miss Meredith," said the agent, "will you have the kindness to step this way? And Jackson, don't go just yet; I shall want you."

A step on the stairs,—another manager! This time a tall, thin man, with a snake-like expression, entered, one of those persons towards whom one feels an antipathy at first sight; and yet he was not without a certain amount of fascination, producing the kind of feeling a serpent exercises over a bird. His manners were smooth and insinuating, and looking round the room with a smile, and recognising several faces he knew, he crossed over to them, and to judge from the giggling and laughing that ensued, was one of the most amiable of men.

"Will you step this way, if you please, Mr. Somers," said the agent, reappearing, and addressing the manager. "I am extremely sorry to keep you waiting, but there are so many managers in town."

"Don't mention it; I have only been here a few minutes, and with such a galaxy of beauty, should think hours short had I the time."

With this charming compliment he entered the private room. In a few moments the door opened, and the agent beckoned to Cora. She could scarcely stand, she was so nervous; but there was no time to be lost, so she entered.

"This is the young lady, I think, who will suit you for utility," said the agent.

"Have you ever been on the stage, my dear?" enquired Mr. Somers.

"Yes," said Cora, "in the *ballet* at Drury Lane."

"Ah! and you want to be an actress; a very laudable ambition, and a deuced pretty one you'll make, if you take pains and study. If you've any talent we'll bring it out, Miss What's-your-name."

"Wilton," said Cora. "Cora Wilton."

"That is a pretty name; what made you choose it?"

"It's my own," said Cora.

"Oh! your own, is it? Well then, Miss Wilton, you would really like to come to me for the utility?"

"Yes," said Cora, "if you think I am fit to take it."

"Very well, we'll consider it settled. I don't open for the summer season weeks, but rehearsals commence before, and I expect all my company to meet on the stage on the fourth of May, just five weeks from now. We shall close next week for the winter," said Mr. Somers to the Agent, "and the opera comes for Easter, so we shall have a very short recess this year."

"Well, Miss Wilton, will you have the kindness to come here on Thursday? The engagement shall be ready for you to sign. And now we will not detain you any longer, so good morning, and mind you take care of yourself."

With this parting injunction, Cora left the agent's private sanctum. She was passing through the outer room as quickly as possible, when she was startled by her name being called, and on turning to see who it was that claimed her acquaintance, recognised Ella Graham. She was very pleased to see her, and anxious to hear what she was going to do, so readily acceded to Ella's request that she should wait and accompany her part of the way home.

"Ah! my dear," said the Agent, again entering the outer room, "I'm glad you are in time; we were just talking about you. Better come in at once."

This was addressed to Ella, who did as desired, and in a few moments reappeared, and, together with Cora, left the office.

When they gained the street Ella said, "So, Cora, we are to be friends, for I find we are both going to Elmerton."

"I'm so glad," cried Cora, "but what are you going to do?"

"Act, to be sure; did you think I couldn't? Why, when I was a little girl, I used often to play small parts, although dear mamma could not endure my doing so. But there; do not let us talk about that. Tell me what you have been doing since I saw you last."

Cora told all the news of the theatre, passing over all mention of Sir Reginald, and her estrangement from her friend, Ellen Morris. When she had finished, Ella was silent for a few moments, and then said, "How good-hearted those girls are, Cora; even Kate. What should I have done but for their kindness, when I sprained my foot that night, and although I hope to pay the money back, I can never forget their goodness. Have you anything particular to do to-day? Because, if not, come and have some tea with me. Mamma and Eunice will be very glad to see you, for I have talked a great deal about you. It is rather a long way, but we will have an early tea, and walk part of the way back with you."

Cora made some excuse about her mother's anxiety, but her curiosity to see Mrs. Graham and Eunice overcame her scruples, and she accompanied Ella home. Mrs. Graham received her daughter's friend with great kindness.

The Grahames lodged in a house of humble appearance, kept by an old woman, who made a small shop of the downstairs room, for the sale of periodicals, and let the two top ones to Ella's mother. By these means she managed to support herself and grandchild, a boy of nine years, whose mother and father had been dead some time.

Ella's friend was welcomed by Mrs. Graham. She was a woman of not more than thirty-eight, with a pale, careworn, refined expression, and large, dark eyes, like Ella's. Her figure was tall and elegant. She gave the idea of one who had lived through some fearful sorrow; yet one could not help thinking how fascinating she must have been. Little Eunice, the other occupant, was a pale, slender child, of weird appearance, with dark eyes like her mother's, but an immense quantity of pale, flaxen hair. She was mournful-looking, thoughtful, and quiet, far beyond her years. The little room was neat, though poor, and a few small things about showed the refinement of its tenants. The only article of real value was a small miniature on ivory set in gold, hung over the fire place, which Mrs. Graham, in all her poverty, had still retained. It represented a young man of aristocratic appearance, with a striking resemblance to Ella.

There was a mystery about Mrs. Graham's first marriage, that people had not been able to solve; so, of course, as there was nothing known, there were many rumours, some most absurd. The one thing only known for certain was that Mrs. Graham, when a young girl of seventeen, made her first appearance on the stage, and created a great sensation. Both her parents were in the profession, and never rising above mediocrity themselves, felt very proud of their pretty and clever daughter. When she had been following her profession for a year, she suddenly disappeared, and no trace could be found of her for four years, when she as suddenly reappeared, accompanied by a little girl of three years; but the beautiful Eva Graham was indeed altered. Not that she was less beautiful, but a storm seemed to have passed over her, that had taken away all her youth and joyousness, and left the cares and staidness of premature age. She was still clever, but no longer as the charming girl that won her audience; it was now the woman who had suffered. Great was the general curiosity to solve the mystery, but that person would have been bold indeed who dared look in Eva Graham's face, and question her. So she resumed her profession, and things went on quietly for the lapse of six years, when it was her misfortune to take a provincial engagement, and there meet a tragedian named Lawrence. He was a man of great personal beauty, and fascinating manners, and soon became enamoured of the beautiful, cold actress, upon whom no one could make an impression; and determined to win her. But he found the task harder than he had imagined. However, he succeeded at last in gaining her consent to his suit. No one could tell why; but they were married, and then commenced a life of torture. Hidden under the handsome exterior, was a nature, coarse, brutal, and cruel. Little Ella, who had never even seen a theatre, was sent on the stage by her stepfather. The wretched mother fought against it, but she was compelled to consent at last, for the sake of keeping her child. The man determined to work no more, but to make his wife and child support him in his life of vice

3

and wretchedness. Here was a sad fate for the proud
Eva; but continual fretting and cruel treatment at last
prevailed. After the birth of her second child, Eunice,
she had never recovered her strength; and when it was
four years old, she caught a cold that deprived her of her
voice. Though it seemed a fearful calamity, it was in
reality a great blessing, for, being unable to follow her
profession, she could no longer support her brutal husband; so, after taking what things he could, he one day
deserted her. Sad poverty resulted; but even that was
better than cruelty and blows; and in time Ella managed
to support her mother and sister out of her professional
earnings, so that life became endurable: but the expression of deep sorrow never passed out of the mother's
fair face.

Knowing nothing of this strange story, Cora was
simply impressed by the woman's kindness, seconded by
that of Ella, but all the evening she thought what a
beautiful woman Mrs. Graham must have been, wondering all the way home what the sorrow could have been
to leave that sad expression on her features. "Perhaps,"
thought Cora, "her first husband died, but then people
would have known his name. No, that cannot be," and
finding other conjectures just as unlikely, gave up specu-
lating on the subject, and reverted to her all-absorbing
thought, Sir Reginald.

"I am to see him to-morrow," she exclaimed; "I
really will tell him that I cannot see him again until I
have told mamma, but then I do love him so very, very
dearly, and he is so good and noble, and so unhappy.
When we are married I will make him very happy, and
he shall never regret marrying me. Mamma will look
so pretty, beautifully dressed as she used to be, and how
pleased she will be to live with her daughter, Lady Clayton. What a grand name, to be sure!"

Cora was so busy building her airy castles, that the
way home, instead of being very long, seemed quite a
short distance. Her mother was rather alarmed at her
absence, but on hearing her account of the day, forgot to
scold her for her thoughtlessness, and Cora, pleading

fatigue from her long walk, retired early to bed, to dream of being a great actress, and passing through most wonderful adventures, but becoming Lady Clayton at last.

CHAPTER V

DISENCHANTMENT.

"A WET day, I declare," said Sir Reginald, as he pulled aside the curtains from his window and surveyed the street, looking as only a London street can look on a wet day, "and no chance of its clearing, so far as I can see. What a deuced nuisance! Of course that child can't come out, her mother won't let her, and there will be no knowing when I shall have the opportunity of seeing her again. However, it cannot be helped, and I will go on the chance of her being there."

So after breakfasting and dressing with great care, one of his usual habits, no matter where he was going, he sent for a Hansom. Arrived at Waterloo Bridge, he dismissed his cab, and armed with an umbrella, prepared to brave the rain. He had not long to wait, for Cora had managed, by some excuse, to keep her appointment in spite of the weather. This interview was much the same as the previous ones, protestations on the one side, credulity on the other, and ended in the same way, that is, without Cora having sufficient courage to avow her determination of never seeing him again unless with her mother's consent.

"But I will the next time," thought poor Cora to herself, "whatever comes of it. I cannot endure this deceit, and mamma would never breathe a word. Yes, I will tell him so to-night when I see him for the moment he asked me."

Sir Reginald's face on leaving Cora bore anything but an amiable expression, and it was a true index to his feelings, if one might judge from the conversation addressed to the air in which he indulged.

"What a fool I am making of myself running after a little ballet girl!" he ejaculated, "and doing the sentimental just like an unfledged strippling. It must be settled; Cora shall be mine at once, for the affair is getting too ridiculous, and if it gets known, I shall be laughed at by all the town. Yes, this very night I will ask her to fly with me; that is the term I must use, I suppose, for the girl is, or pretends to be, so preciously romantic. However, some way or other it must be arranged."

*　　*　　*　　*　　*　　*

The evening came that was to change poor Cora's happiness into sorrow. Sir Reginald, true to his resolution of the morning, urged Cora to fly with him, but she told him that much as she loved him, it was impossible to marry him without her mother's consent.

"But Cora, dearest," he urged, "why talk of marriage? it is the grave of love."

This was the first time she had ever heard such a sentiment, and for a while her pure mind could not comprehend it, but when at last she grasped the wickedness and perfidy, it struck her dumb with anguish. Her silence Sir Reginald attributed to quite another cause; and having, as he expressed it, broken the ice, he urged his suit with intensity. But Cora hardly heard him. The one thing, the death-knell to all her hopes, kept ringing in her ears, "Why talk of marriage, the grave of love?" Now, indeed, she was punished for her deceit to her mother, and by the man whom she had thought so good, so honourable. At last she found her voice, and turning her face to Sir Reginald, fairly startled him by the agony of its expression. The young childish face seemed in those few moments to grow almost old, so altered did it look.

"It seems, Sir Reginald, we have both been mistaken in each other," she said. "I have invested you with a noble, honourable character you did not possess, and you thought the girl who deceived her mother must be ripe for any infamy, however black. It is a noble action, truly, to fascinate and win the love of a foolish girl for no other purpose than to trample on it. I have been mad, infatuated, but never can stoop to infamy. Thank you for opening my eyes ; I would not marry you now, even did you do me the honour to ask me, to save my life. No, Sir Reginald, the ballet girl despises you, and thus for ever will I, even at the cost of my life, tear you from my memory."

Saying this, she took the ring he had given her, and threw it on the ground, and left him rooted to the spot, with surprise and shame. Yes, shame, for in spite of, as he thought, the theatrical language, he knew that it was true, and that he had lost for ever the love of Cora.

As he wended his way home that night, his breast was a prey to conflicting sensations,—hate, revenge, shame, and love, racked him by turns, for now he knew Cora was lost to him for ever he felt a fierce love spring up in his heart which he knew could never be appeased. Already his torment had begun : in seeking to ruin that girlish heart, he had lost his own, and the knowledge came as a punishment ; henceforth he must carry about with him the knowledge that his own wickedness had converted, what might have been his greatest blessing, into a heavy burden, for his nature was a strong one, and the love, he knew, instead of diminishing, would go on increasing, and the thought that at some future time Cora should love again, was fairly maddening to him. And how fared it with Cora ? Ah, poor child ! could her greatest enemies have seen her as she sat in her own room, where she had retired on pretence of a head-ache, they would have pitied her. It was her first great sorrow, and whatever might happen to her in after life, nothing could equal it in intensity of suffering. She had loved and trusted, and the being she had invested with every virtue, she found but clay and full of flaws. Poor Cora ! now, indeed, all joyousness was crushed out of that young heart.

CHAPTER VI.

LEAVING HOME.

THREE weeks had elapsed since Cora's last interview with Sir Reginald, and, although he had tried several times to see her, she had always managed to avoid him; she felt that she could not bear the pain of meeting him. After what had passed, she loved him no longer; indeed it may be doubted whether she ever really loved Sir Reginald. The idol she worshipped, with all the fervour of her girlish love, was a being of her own imagining; her ideal of all that was good and noble, and when she discovered the reality, her heart might break for the past, but she could never love one so unworthy. The Sir Reginald she had loved was good and great, but the Sir Reginald of that last interview would never have won her love.

Still the wound was fresh, and Cora could not therefore endure to see the man who had inflicted it. She was restless and unhappy, anxiously looking forward to the time when her engagement should take her away from London and her own sad thoughts.

"Next Tuesday I shall leave London," she said to herself; "how long these weeks have been—I thought they would never pass; how glad I shall be when Tuesday comes, and yet I shall leave home for the first time in my life. What an ungrateful girl I am to dear mamma and papa, after all their love and care."

This thought so overcame poor Cora, that she threw herself on her bed, and burst into an uncontrollable fit of tears.

At last Tuesday arrived, and Cora bade adieu to her

parents, and, in company with Ella Graham, journeyed
to Elmerton. What a number of strange faces crowded
through Cora's brain during the journey ! It was almost
the first time she had travelled by rail, and now she was
going to a strange place among strangers, and yet in
spite of leaving friends and home, she was happier than
she had been since the night of her great sorrow.

"Elmerton at last," said Ella ; "I thought we should
never arrive. What a dreadful long journey ; I am
almost tired to death."

"I have not found it so tiresome," said Cora ; "but
what are we to do now we are here ?"

"Why, leave our luggage at the station for the present, and go straight to the theatre. They are sure to
have a list of apartments to let in the hall, and we can
take down the names of a few, and go and see them."

This resolution was adopted, and they left the station
on their voyage of discovery.

"Can you direct us the nearest way to the theatre ?"
Ella asked of a country bumpkin, who happened to be
passing at the time.

"The theaytre ? oh that be some way from here, more
nor half a mile ; but if you go straight, and then ask
again you'll sure to find it."

With this valuable information they were obliged to
be content, and in spite of many difficulties the theatre
was reached at last.

"Have you a list of apartments ?" said Ella to the
doorkeeper, who was there from ten until six to receive
letters and transact other business.

"Yes, Miss ; what kind do you want ? There's Mrs.
Green, at Waterloo Cottage ; she's got two pretty little
rooms to let. Our leading lady had them last year, and
said she had never been so comfortable in all her life."

Cora felt her spirits fail at the mention of the leading
lady, because she was quite sure they would be very
expensive, but Ella thought otherwise, and decided to
see them. Waterloo Cottage was very near the theatre,
and certainly scarcely deserved so grand a name, for a

more shabby little place it would be difficult to find. However, it might be better inside, and if a leading lady could live there, of course they could, so they knocked at the door. A cross, untidy-looking girl opened it, and she, in answer to their inquiries, screamed, "Mother, here's some ladies wants to see the lodgings." A fat, jolly-looking woman made her appearance, wiping the soap suds from her arms, and began a long string of apologies at keeping them waiting. "But it's washing day, and that Sarah Ann is the idlest girl, and never can show the rooms."

Poor Ella and Cora followed the loquacious landlady into a small parlour, so small indeed that it looked as though it had been built expressly for inconvenience.

"This is the sitting-room, and this," throwing open a door, and disclosing an apartment of even smaller dimensions, "is the bed-room."

The two girls murmured that the rooms were a trifle small, but Mrs. Green looked astonished, and said "the beauty of them was their cosy look, besides they were so nice and warm."

Cora thought that hardly a recommendation in the summer, but felt too tired to hazard the remark, and on the landlady stating that she would take seven and sixpence a week, urged Ella to decide in favour of them.

"Please, ladies," said Mrs. Green, as she took the bill out of the window, "don't mention at the theaytre that I have took seven and sixpence a-week, because it would hurt me, for last year Miss St. Clare paid me eight and six; but now, ladies, shall I send for your luggage? And I dare say you'll be glad of a cup of tea, so if you tell me what you want, that Sarah Ann shall go and get the things."

Ella gave Mrs. Green the desired information, and she sallied forth to execute her young lodgers' wishes, very pleased with her good fortune in letting her rooms before her rival, Mrs. Stubbs, at Victoria Villa, near at hand.

"Mind, Sarah Ann," she said, "get a quarter of a

pound of the best mixed tea, and call at the butcher's, and ask for two nice chops off the chump end, they can have some of our sugar and bread to-day, so look sharp ; but, Sarah Ann, don't forget if you see Mrs. Stubbs's Eliza to tell her we are let to the two first ladies at the theaytre."

When Mrs. Green had left the room, Cora had time to look round and examine her new home, if it could be so called. The sitting-room was twelve feet by ten, with folding doors opening into the bed-room, the floor was covered with a bright, red carpet of gigantic pattern ; a round table, and four bright stained wood chairs to represent mahogany, together with a glass over the mantel shelf, which had the delightful tendency of impressing you with the idea that your face was a little smaller and bilious, completed the furniture of the room, if we except two oil paintings of the landlady and her husband,—not a very cheerful room to pass your spare time in, but it was cheap, and that was a very great recommendation to Ella and Cora. " We shall soon be very happy here," said the former, noticing Cora's downcast look ; "when we get a few flowers and one thing and another, it is astonishing how much a place improves, and the landlady seems a good-natured creature, so cheer up, dear, and after tea we will go for a little walk, before going to bed. To-morrow, you know, we must look our best, for the company meet on the stage at twelve, so we had better go to bed early or we shall look tired in the morning, and that will never do."

Cora yielded to the higher and more cheerful views of her friend, and the first evening in their new lodgings passed not unpleasantly.

Next morning at twelve precisely, Ella and Cora, dressed in the best their wardrobe provided, presented themselves at the theatre. They were almost the first, and after putting down their names and address in a book kept by the doorkeeper, they were conducted on to the stage. It was so dark, that at first Cora could scarcely see, but in a few moments a gentleman came up and introduced himself as Mr. Lexham, the stage manager.

"Come with me, ladies," said he, "and I will show you the green-room; some of the company have arrived, so you will have an opportunity of making their acquaintance before the piece is read. Mind that step, it is very awkward! I don't know of what use it is, except to break one's legs over; but here we are. By the bye, I don't know the names of the ladies I have the pleasure of pioneering."

"Miss Wilton and Miss Graham," said Ella.

"Here is the green-room," rejoined their guide.

It was a strange scene that met the gaze of our heroine—a rather large room, covered with a well-worn carpet, with seats ranged round the walls, a large looking-glass, and sundry stage properties, in the shape of gilded chairs and tables, too large to be stowed away in the property-room; but if the room had little to interest one, it was not so with the company. Cora had never been in a country theatre before, and the marked difference between the London professional and his provincial brother struck her with amazement; in place of the elegant and fashionable attire she had been used to see during her short theatrical career, here were thread-bare coats and napless hats, and even a more extraordinary style of dress prevailed among the ladies.

But before she had time to notice much, Mr. Lexham took her up to a large lady in a very fine bonnet, saying, "Allow me to introduce you to Mrs. Lexham, Miss Wilton."

"Delighted to see you, my dear," said Mrs. Lexham, making room beside her for Cora; "and so you are going to join us? Why, I think you, your friend, and Mr. Taunton are the only new people we have, all the rest are our old company. What is your line of business, my dear?"

"Oh, I have only come to play little parts," said Cora; "but Miss Graham, my friend, has come for first walking lady."

"Indeed! Graham did you say her name was? Is she any relation to Eva Graham, do you know?"

"Yes, her daughter."

"You don't say so," said Mrs. Lexham, in quite an excited tone. "Why, I remember her mother years ago; I was in the theatre when she made her first appearance, and that girl's grandmother was a very dear friend of mine; we travelled together on the same circuit several years. Bring her to me, my dear, I shall be very glad to know her, and if she has only a quarter of her mother's talent, she will be a great acquisition to our company."

Ella was introduced, and was in the middle of a most animated conversation, when the manager entered with a roll of papers, and, after bowing to the company, seated himself at a small table. Silence now fell on the occupants of the room, which was broken by the manager selecting a paper and calling for Mr. Maddox. A tall thin man, about thirty-five years of age, answered to the name. "This is your part," said the manager; "it is a very good one, quite original."

With this observation, he turned to a list of names he had in his hand, and called Miss Lenster. A rather pretty woman, in a very dowdy dress, answered, and received her part, only remarking that it seemed very long. Miss Graham's name was the next, and Ella going forward, took her part in silence. All the parts were distributed, except one, and Cora was beginning to think she would not be required to play in the new piece, when her name was called. She went, like the others, to receive it, and the manager gave it to her with a smile.

"Here is a very nice little part for you, which I am sure you will act charmingly. And now, ladies and gentlemen, good morning. Lexham, call a rehearsal to-morrow morning for this piece at eleven."

A perfect Babel succeeded the manager's disappearance, each one giving his or her opinion of the piece, and these opinions being favourable, or otherwise, according to the goodness of the parts, were rather numerous and singular.

"I," said Mr. Maddox, the leading man, "think the piece, as far as I can see, bosh; there is only one good situation in my part; and that is not so very great, after all. Why, in the 'Murderer's Mother,' last season, there were three, all better than this one."

"Well," said Miss Lenster, "I have only looked at my part; but I should think the piece is very good."

"Oh, no doubt! you have all the cream," observed Mr. Maddox.

"What says Miss Martin? Is the chamber-maid equally good?"

Miss Martin, a pretty, merry girl, replied with a laugh:

"In this charming production my part seems all right; but how you grumble. It's really a pity; if a piece is not entirely written for the leading names, they always make such a fuss."

Cora only having been in the ballet at Drury Lane, and that during the pantomime, had never before seen the way a new piece is received, and she was quite astonished, and longed to see what she had to do in this apple of discord, and, bowing to Mr. Lexham, left the room unperceived, so great was the excitement produced.

On reaching Waterloo Cottage, she divested herself of her bonnet, and sat down to read her part. It was not long, but she found it so interesting that she quite longed to see the piece rehearsed; it was really a good part, and one that suited her character, so she determined to do her best to render it well and faithfully. In a short time, Ella returned, equally pleased; and the young girls ate their frugal meal and discussed the relative attractions of each member of the company to their mutual satisfaction.

CHAPTER VII.

IN THE ETERNAL CITY.

WHEN Sir Reginald found that Cora had really left London, he was furious, and determined to leave no stone unturned to discover her; but the days passed without success, so often does it happen that you may search far and wide, and yet, after all, the person you are seeking may be your next-door neighbour. The "Theatre Royal," Elmerton, was not of sufficient importance to advertise, except in the strictly theatrical papers, and then not the names of its company, so Sir Reginald, although he scanned the advertisement pages with great anxiety daily, had no idea that Cora was living not ten miles from the Towers. How eager he would have been to visit his sister Maud, had he known that the bird he was seeking so unceasingly had alighted so near to his ancestral hall. As it was, not being aware of the fact, he determined to scour England rather than not find her: for now that he understood the nature of his own feeling, he felt indeed that life without her was impossible.

His first journey he decided should be to Liverpool, because he argued she would only go to the theatres in large towns where the London ballet generally went, never for one moment assuming that Cora's ambition had already taken her out of that body. To Liverpool he accordingly went, and after visiting all the theatres without success, turned his steps towards Manchester. It was his first visit to the great trade emporium of England, and he found much to amuse him; but no place could interest him long, and after running half over England, he decided in a fit of disgust to go on the Continent, and see if a course of dissipation would not drive Cora out of his thoughts. He accordingly returned to London, and bidding Adolphe pack his things and accompany him, started for Paris that very night. Sir Reginald was well-known in the gay city, and he received if not a cordial at least a noisy reception ; and if beauty could distract his thoughts from Cora there was no lack of it among his fair friends, who were all ready to fight for his heart, or rather his purse ; but though he plunged into the very depths of wild Parisian life, he could not buy forgetfulness. After a time, therefore, Paris growing triste to him, he left his friends to console themselves as best they could for his unceremonious departure, and started for Italy. Florence he found intolerable, and hurried thence to Rome. He had never before cared to see that city. His was not one of those natures that love the grand and beautiful, and although he had spent years of his life in the other cities of Europe, Rome had never possessed attractions for him. But now finding every other place distasteful, he thought of Rome, and imagined that a new scene might help to dispel the ennui under which he was labouring.

It was a beautiful bright morning when he entered on the glorious Compagnia, with its moss-like verdure, and dark-blue mountains in the distance, dotted here and there with the monumental remains of human greatness. Even his worldly nature was touched for the moment, purified by the loveliness of the scene.

"What a fool I have been," said he to himself, "not to come here before, I had no idea of the beauty of Rome."

A few moments and the station was reached. What a Babel of voices, and what numbers of carriages, the owners all eager to take the Signor! "What hotel did he mean to go to?" asked his valet; "the Hotel de l'Europe was one of the best." Then to the Hotel de l'Europe he decided to go, and was soon rolling along in a two-horse carriage to the Piazza de Spagna, where the hotel is situated.

If the country struck him as being beautiful, the city equally astounded him with its ancient appearance, so unlike any other that he had ever visited. It gave one the idea of just having awakened from a thousand years' sleep, and one could almost imagine one had gone back two or three centuries away from this matter-of-fact age with all its prosy realities. Sir Reginald was awakened from a reverie of this kind by arriving at the hotel; he had heard so much against Roman comfort that he was most agreeably disappointed to find the Hotel de l'Europe one of the most comfortable ones he had ever visited; and after partaking of a good breakfast, sallied forth to see Rome. He strolled down the Via Condotti into the Corso, and having duly admired the beauty of some of the palaces, called a one-horse vehicle and started for St. Peter's. He had to cross the Tiber by the Ponto Angelo, and everything around him had some interest. On that bridge Beatrice Cenci suffered death; and that grand old castle on the other side, with the French flag flying on its ramparts, had witnessed many a brilliant pageant and direful tragedy since the day it was built for Hadrian's tomb. St. Peter's was at length reached; he entered it almost an atheist, and thoroughly imbued with the material views of this unbelieving age, bowed down in his heart before the glorious faith that could make men raise such an edifice to the glory of the God they worshiped. For a moment Sir Reginald felt that had he been taught to believe, his fate might have been wholly different; but it was too late to think of these things, he argued; besides it was all superstition, and as he had begun, so he must go on. The world had too great a hold over him.

"This will never do," said he, " I shall begin moralizing if I stop here. I can quite understand people believing all sorts of uncomfortable things if they remain here; but if it should be true after all, and not a myth that there is an hereafter? But why do I think about it? I declare, if I stop here, I shall be converted, as the parsons call it, so I will bid adieu to this dangerous building, and find something more cheerful to think about."

Looking at his watch, he found that he had just time to return to the hotel to lunch before he went on the Pincian to see the fashionable world. After luncheon, finding that the Pincian was very near, he walked down to

it, and there had the good fortune to meet an old acquaintance. Together they stood against the rails, and criticised
the beauties as they rolled by on the Roman Rotten Row.
There were natives of all climes ; the golden-haired
English girl ; the sparkling French woman ; and the
large, languid, dark Roman bella donna. Then the men
who lounged against the rails were from all countries ;
the German, heavy and fair ; the Englishman, with his
yellow moustaches and his listless air ; and the Roman
youths, all of the same type, with lithe, panther-like form,
glorious dark eyes, and faultlessly fitting clothes.

"I say, Merton, who are those?" said Sir Reginald, as
a carriage containing two ladies passed.

"Oh! Austrians. Every one is talking about them ;
they are thought very lovely, but I like something more
like women, and less like stone. I met them the other
night at a ball at the French Embassy, and got introduced, but never met such slow girls. They are certainly
very beautiful, but that is all. Now, that girl (as a
splendid chariot rolled by, and a bright face bent forward
to bow to Mr. Merton) is worth a dozen of the other two
to my mind ; she is charming. Hers is rather a strange
history. About eight years back—so says rumour—she
was a flower girl in Paris, and the old Baron de Leignie
saw her, fell in love with, educated, and married her, but
died in less than a year afterwards, leaving her the whole
of his property ; she has been a widow four years, and
although well known in every court in Europe, no one
has ever succeeded in winning her, and her greatest
enemy cannot accuse her of the slightest indiscretion,
although she has admiration and homage enough to turn
any woman's head wherever she goes. But I say,
Clayton, whatever brought you to the Eternal City? I
thought you had registered a vow against ever visiting
it ?"

"I don't exactly know what put the idea into my
head," was the reply, "but finding every place slow, I
thought I would just see Rome ; and I am very glad I have
come, for, upon my word, I think it is very jolly. I had no
idea it was so nice. But what do you do in the evening?"

"Oh! plenty of balls, and so on. But the season is nearly over; in a week or ten days Rome will be almost empty; you should have come a month ago. It is getting almost too hot now. What a bore it is that you cannot stay in the summer, for I think no place so beautiful. I don't know how it is, but somehow or other Rome exercises a peculiar fascination over me, and I cannot live away from it. Year after year I come back to meet the same faces, and do the same things. I am far more at home in it than in London; and when I return the very stones seem like old friends, and welcome me back. I always look forward with pleasure to coming, and with regret to leaving. I have no doubt you will catch the Roman epidemic, as we call it, now you have come this once," said Mr. Merton, "but I never expected to find Rome so amusing. By the way, will you dine with me to-day, and go to the opera? I have a box, and the ballet is perfectly charming"

Sir Reginald agreed, and after walking round the Pincian two or three times, went home to his hotel to dress.

The two friends having dined together at Merton's rooms in the Corso, went to the opera at the Theatre Torlonia, or Apollo, as it is called. The beauty of the house quite surprised Sir Reginald; for, although small in comparison with the opera houses of other towns in Italy, its tasteful and light decorations gave it a most charming effect, and Sir Reginald was in a humour to be pleased with anything. The opera he pronounced excellent, although really not above mediocrity, and the *ballet* (which came after the second act of the opera, the usual thing in Rome, because they consider the *ballet* far before the music), he declared he had never seen equalled, and for the time even Cora was forgotten.

So the evening passed rapidly away. The *ballet* was over, and Sir Reginald declining Mr. Merton's invitation to supper with a few friends of his, returned to his hotel, well pleased with his first day in the Eternal City. Adolphe was waiting to assist him in undressing, and his master astonished him by his familiarity, asking him how

4

he liked Rome, and what he had been doing with himself all day. Adolphe was too wise and crafty a servant not to take his cue from his master, and seeing that Sir Reginald was really pleased, expressed himself delighted with all he had seen.

When dismissed for the night, Adolphe went to his own room, and opening a small iron-clasped box, took from it a parcel (having previously taken the precaution to lock the door), and proceeded to undo it. The contents were of a very singular description. First a paper in which was wrapped a long dark curl of hair; then a blood-stained handkerchief and little dagger; and lastly, a small miniature.

For some moments the man seemed quite overcome at the sight of these relics of the past, but conquering his emotion, he looked long and earnestly at the picture, which represented a very pretty French peasant girl of the southern type.

"Ah! Marie," said the man, addressing the picture in his hand, "you shall be avenged. Little does the villain who caused your death think that I, Adolphe, his valet, the slave of his caprices, have sworn to take his worthless life. I would have taken it long ago, but that would not be revenge enough for me! No, I wanted him to suffer some of the pangs he has caused me to feel. He has a sister whom he loves: not more beautiful nor more innocent than you were, Marie, when the tempter first saw you; but she is too faithfully guarded, and although many a time I have stolen forth to take her life, something has withheld me. And now I am rewarded. He loves another with all his black devotion, and through her I will wring his heart."

Uttering these words with fierce intensity, Adolphe restored the picture and other things to their hiding-place.

And how fared Sir Reginald? Was there no guardian angel to warn him of his danger? Alas! no. But his dreams were strange. He thought he was in a little village in southern France, a young student; but, alas! even there, deeply versed in crime; and a well-remembered form, long since forgotten, was by his side; it was that of a young girl, the daughter of an innkeeper, called the belle of the village. She was listening to vows of love. When he first came to her father's house, an invalid, she had nursed him, and insensibly grew to love her patient with the passionate love only felt in a southern breast, and no wonder her emotion almost overcame her to find her love returned—she a poor innkeeper's daughter and he a great English noble! It seemed impossible; but, then, love "levels all distinctions," and since many a noble had married a peasant maiden, why should not her lot be equally bright? Alas! poor Marie, he is too true a scion of his wicked race to make you his bride, even though you have beauty, innocence, and a true heart for your dowry,—jewels beyond price, but worthless to such a nature as Sir Reginald Clayton's.

His dream changes. He is standing by a river, and his companion is the same girl, but now how changed! Her face is haggard with agony, while he is calmly indifferent.

"Why make all this fuss?" he says at last; "I shall come back soon, and you could not have been so mad as to think I really meant to make you my wife! If you will only keep your own counsel all will be well."

"Oh! Holy Virgin, what shall I do?" moaned the poor creature. "I cannot live with this disgrace, and you no longer love me! Only three short months ago I was a happy, innocent girl, and now my sin and sorrow are more than I can bear. Farewell for ever!"

The scene again shifts. He is standing with a crowd of people in a small room. On the bed poor Marie lies, cold and lifeless, stabbed by her own hand, with a little dagger of curious workmanship which he had given her. Yes! by that weapon she had let her sorrow-laden soul free! He well remembered the horror he felt and the haste with which he quitted the village, leaving everything but his purse behind, and somehow Adolphe seemed mixed up with his dream, and he awoke in a state of fear and terror.

The sun was shining brightly into his room, and feeling

no wish to renew the phantasies, he arose and dressed himself, and finding it was still too early for his breakfast, strolled out, eager to dispel the unpleasant effects his dreams had occasioned in his mind. But do what he would he could not shake off the feeling of oppression and remorse. Even in the worst natures that little voice of conscience will make itself heard, in spite of all the efforts made to stifle it, and now Sir Reginald was experiencing the truth of this. The events causing him such bitter pangs had happened years before, and he had almost forgotten them; but here they were awakened to fearful vitality by a dream.

" Poor little Marie," he said, as he walked along, "how fondly you loved me! I was a great brute; but what could I have done to prevent it? Yet for all that I would give ten years of my life could I blot that page from it. But, pshaw! what is the good of making myself miserable about a thing done years ago. It is no use thinking. All the wishing in the world will not bring Marie De la Pierre back again to life; so I will dismiss the subject from my mind."

It was easy to say this, but in spite of all his endeavours, the face of the dead Marie would rise up before him, and finding that walking alone, instead of dispelling his dreams, only made them more vivid, he returned to breakfast. Adolphe was ready to receive him, and made many apologies at not being down to dress Sir Reginald; " but you were up so early, sir," he said. No one to look in that man's quiet, immovable face would think of the burning passions in his breast. As Sir Reginald looked into it, he fancied he saw there a likeness to the lost Marie. " But it cannot be," he said to himself; "I am getting quite demented."

During breakfast Sir Reginald resolved to try the distraction of the picture galleries, but finding they did not open until twelve, he thought a drive out on the Compagnia would do him good. With this view he left the town by the Porta Pia, and visited the beautiful old church of St. Agnese. He almost laughed at the idea of the gay Sir Reginald finding any delight in such simple pleasures, but somehow or other they seemed to soothe him, and did more to dissipate the phantoms of the night than anything else could have done. On reaching his hotel, he found on his dressing-table a card, for a ball that night, enclosed in a note from Mr. Merton. "Do come, old fellow," said the note; "it's a very short notice, but I am sure you will enjoy it, and as it is almost the last of the season, you will have no other opportunity of meeting the beautiful Austrians or my divine baroness."

"Yes, I will go," said Sir Reginald, "and see if I can drive these thoughts out of my head; those Austrians are beautiful, but not to be compared with Cora. What a sensation she would make in the fashionable world, with those magical eyes and bewitching smile. Heigh ho! the fascination the little witch exercises over me! There is such a thing as real love, and I am labouring under a severe attack of it. I have always laughed at the idea, but now——"

"You will come, old fellow, won't you?" said the voice of Mr. Merton, as he walked into the room. "But what the deuce is the matter with you? Why, man, you look as though you had seen a ghost! You have not got an attack of the Roman fever, have you?"

"Oh, no," replied Sir Reginald, with a forced smile; "I did not have a very good night, and that always knocks me up."

"Well let us go for a gallop on the Compagnia. That will do you good. You can get a very tolerable hack at Farrett's, where I keep my own horse, so come along and we will go together; a ride will do neither of us any harm."

The ball that Sir Reginald was going to that night was the last of a series of entertainments given by a French nobleman, and was to surpass all the former ones in splendour and extravagance.

All the rank and fashion of Rome were invited, and many had deferred their departure from the Eternal City, on purpose to be present at this ball. It was early for Rome when Sir Reginald and Mr. Merton

entered the palace of the Marquis de Leon, and, although
the former had assisted at fêtes of almost unexampled
extravagance, both in London and Paris, never had such
a scene of enchantment burst upon his sight.

The courtyards of the old palace were turned into
fairyland, and one expected to see the fairies themselves
come forth from the endless confusion of flowers that
perfumed the air to greet the presumptuous mortals who
dared profane by their presence the enchanted scene.
The two friends sat down in a corner, and Mr. Merton
gave Sir Reginald sketches of the guests as they entered.
At last the Austrians arrived, followed by the Baroness
de Leignie, so our friends thought it time to enter the
ball-room. If the courts and gardens formed a scene of
enchantment, what can be said of the ball-room? It
dazzled and bewildered, embellished as it was with the
superb toilettes of the women and gorgeous uniforms of
the men.

"Come along, Clayton, let me introduce you to the
baroness," said Merton.

And before Sir Reginald had time to speak, the intro-
duction was over, and he was listening to the silver
tones of the fair baroness's voice. When he had seen her
on the Pincian, she had not struck him as being such a
great beauty, but a few moments in her society and he
ceased to wonder at Merton's infatuation or the world's
homage. Virginie de Leignie was far from being the
most beautiful woman in that room, as far as mere
beauty of feature and colouring went, but when she
spoke, few men could withstand her fascination. Her
voice had a peculiar silvery tone (unlike her country
manner generally) that charmed the hearer, and her face
lit up with a magical power, giving even the most trivial
thing she uttered an interest. Sir Reginald felt himself
irresistibly interested in the beautiful creature, whose
strange history he had heard from his friend.

"What a singular thing is destiny," said he to himself. "Seven years ago this woman, who is now receiving the admiration and homage of princes, was
selling flowers in the streets of Paris."

CHAPTER VIII.

DESTINY is indeed inscrutable, and even as he spoke
Sir Reginald Clayton was a passive victim, helpless in
the volutes of its mystic coils.

While Sir Reginald had been anxiously reading all
the advertisements, in the hope of gaining news of Cora,
she had been studying and rehearsing her first part.
Let us endeavour to realise the circumstances under
which that part was enacted.

It is the opening night, and there having been an
election in the town, the theatre is quite full, all the
private boxes being occupied by the leading families of
the neighbourhood. The overture is played, and all the
company are in a state of great excitement. The curtain
rises, and the new drama begins. It is rather a sensational piece, but the plot, though somewhat unnatural,
is well marked out. Cora does not appear until the
second act. The act drop falls on the prologue of the
piece: it is a success so far. Now comes the great
point of interest, the debût of Cora, for the bills have
announced that the part of the miner's daughter will be
taken by a young lady who makes her first appearance
on the stage in that character. The curtain again rises.
As Cora enters, she is greeted with loud applause, her
youth and beauty evidently making a great impression
on her audience. At first her voice trembles, but as she
proceeds, she forgets herself and her audience, remembering only that she is the miner's daughter, who will
risk her life for her father's. The part in itself is not a
prominent one, but Cora's natural talent has invested it
with a most intense interest, so true is it that real
genius will shine out no matter what obstacles it has to
overcome. The second act closes amid thunders of applause, and Cora is called before the curtain, and receives
a bouquet from the stage box. She lifts her eyes to see

who has thrown it, and encounters a pair of brown ones intently fixed on her with undisguised admiration. She also observes a lovely girl about her own age, and a middle-aged gentleman, who are the other occupants of the box.

"Is she not lovely, Percy?" says Maud (for she it is whom Cora has noticed in the box).

"Yes, indeed, she is, and a perfect genius," replies Percy, the owner of the brown eyes. "I wonder if she is going to do anything in the third act? Ah! here is another name, we have not seen her yet. Ella Graham! what a grand name."

"Graham!" replies Mr. Walter Earl. "Can it be so! impossible!"

"What is impossible, darling uncle?" cries Maud.

"Nothing, pet, only the name Graham roused some old memories, that is all. But see the curtain rises, and the third act is beginning."

What is it that makes Mr. Earl turn pale, and clutch the edge of his box, as Ella enters for the first time?

"That voice, that face, and then that name—can it be possible that I have been deceived all these years? No, it is only a chance resemblance; and yet the girl is like what Eva was; but, doubtless, were I to see her in the day, all trace of the likeness would be gone, and Graham is a very common name in the theatrical profession. Why, then, should I strive after hopes that can never be realized? No; my love was buried under the blue waters of the Mediterranean, and I am mad to let a name and chance resemblance open old wounds."

And the piece being over, Mr. Earl, after carefully wrapping up his niece, takes her down to the carriage.

"Percy, are you not coming?" cries Maud.

"No, I think I shall stay and see the afterpiece; but I shall be sure to call at the Towers to-morrow; so good night!"

Those are the incidents of Cora's first night; few, but full of interest in the present; full of moment in the future.

Maud thought the ten mile drive home was very dull

and long, but then, to be sure, Percy was not with them, and Uncle Walter was silent, so she was glad when the carriage entered the lodge-gates.

Percy Lysle was Maud's cousin, his mother being a Clayton; but she only lived a few months after the birth of her son, and Herbert Lysle, surviving his wife but a short time, left Percy, a boy two years of age, to the guardianship of his dearest friend, Walter Earl. Mr. Earl had striven hard to fulfil his trust. Percy had strong passions, and a violent temper, counterbalanced, however, by a loving, affectionate, truthful nature; but his was a character that required a mother's watchful care to mould it aright; hence it was no wonder that he had grown up headstrong and impetuous. His minority being so long, and Mr. Earl such a careful guardian, his fortune would be enormous when he came of age; he now wanted one year to that time. It had been only since Mr. Earl's return that he had met his cousin Maud; but, seeing how much Maud liked the society of Percy, Mr. Earl had conceived the idea of uniting those two beings whom he loved best on earth. But, "Man proposes, and God disposes," and the proposal and disposal are not always in accord.

When Percy returned to the box that night, the afterpiece had begun; but the face that had enchanted him appeared no more, and he returned to the Hotel sad and disappointed. He retired to bed, but not to sleep, for the face and form of the little actress haunted him, do what he would, and he arose in the morning feverish and tired with his sleepless night. His first determination was to visit the theatre again that night; but, remembering his promise to Maud, he started for the Towers instead. As he rode along, the bright, fresh morning air did much to alleviate the effects of his restless night; and he arrived at the Towers looking like his wonted self. Maud, sweet Maud, greeted him with smiles of welcome. It was so new for her to have a friend of her own age, that no wonder she gave all the love of her innocent heart to this handsome young cousin. She knew not herself that her feelings towards him were anything

more than of cousinly regard.   And Percy, how did he
look upon this charming relative, whose acquaintance he
had so lately made? Did he love her with a love beyond
mere cousinly affection?   Alas! no; whatever might
have been his first feelings, they were all changed by the
sight of Cora.   She had realised his ideal of all that was
lovely.   However, as the next day he had to return to
College, and could not see Cora before, there was every
chance that, when he again returned, some new divinity
would have obliterated her image from his mind.

Maud was supremely happy, she had so much to talk
to him about respecting the performance of the night
before, and her admiration for Cora was extreme.

"What a darling! was she not, Percy? Do you know
I did not grudge her my bouquet, although you threw it
without asking me, and when she looked up to see where
it came from, her eyes were full of tears.   How clever of
her to act so beautifully.   I could not, if my life de-
pended on it, and she cannot be any older than I am.
You do not know, Percy, how glad I am you have come
so early.   I was so dull.   Uncle Walter I have not seen
this morning.   Is he not naughty to let me breakfast
alone when I had so much to talk about?   Perhaps he
will be back soon, and then I will scold him for taking
such long walks before breakfast, without telling his
Maud that he is going; but, Percy, you have not spoken
a word."

"Well that would be rather difficult, seeing that you
have never given me time to open my mouth since I
arrived."

"Well I declare, Percy, what a dreadful chatterbox I
must be," said Maud, laughing, " but now you can sit
down in the shade and talk for a quarter of an hour, and
I promise not to open my lips once.   See, I can be very
silent; so begin, and tell me if you did not think the
miner's daughter last night very pretty?"

"Yes, Maud, she was pretty, but you forget that there
was another who might be thought more beautiful by
some people."

"Oh, Percy, you do not think so," said Maud, forgetting her vow of silence, " she was very nice, but she looked so sad and mournful, and then it was not her first appearance, you know."

"Oh that is why you admire the fair one with the golden locks, is it? I should have thought, being a blonde yourself, you would rather admire the dark girl. Uncle Walter evidently thought a great deal more of her, for he turned quite pale when she spoke, and seemed ready to faint when she looked up at the box."

"Is that a proof of admiration?" asked Maud archly, " because, if so, what a number of gentlemen must faint when they see a beautiful lady."

"Now, Maud, you have broken your promise to be silent, so I shall punish you by leaving you to see if I can find Uncle Walter."

"Very well," said Maud, "and mind you bring him back to luncheon; I have a great deal to do, so I can spare you very well indeed until then," and Maud skipped blithely away.

It was some time before Percy could find Mr. Earl, but at last he saw him sitting at the foot of a tree, gazing intently at something which he held in his hand. On hearing Percy's footsteps, he rose quickly, and thrusting his hand into his pocket, concealed what he had been looking at from Percy's view.

"Why, Percy, how early you are this morning. Have you seen Maud yet?" said Mr. Earl. "I had a miserable headache, so came out, thinking the fresh air would do me good; but it must be near lunch time, so I think we had better return, Maudie will think we are lost."

Percy saw that Mr. Earl's eyes were red, as if he had been weeping.

"But that is impossible," he thought. "I hate men who cry, and I am sure Uncle Walter is not one of those kind of fellows. Do you not think, uncle," he continued, " that the performance last night was very good for a country theatre?"

"Yes, Percy, but I do not like those sensational pieces; it may be bad taste on my part, but I certainly do not. That little girl who made her *debût* looked pretty and

gentle, almost a child though, not older than our birdie.
What a sad fate! and yet, after all, I daresay she is very
happy, and would not change her life for a great deal;
there must be an immense amount of fascination in public
applause."

Nothing more was said till uncle and nephew reached
the Towers.

" What are you going to do this afternoon till dinner
time?" said Mr. Earl to Percy as they sat at luncheon.

" Why Maud and I have made an arrangement to ride
over to Norton this afternoon, as it is fine, and likely to
be the last ride we shall take together for some
months."

" Ah, true, I forgot that to-morrow you return to
Oxford. Yes, it will do birdie good to have a gallop, but
take care of her, Percy," said Mr. Earl, as Maud ran
away to equip herself for her ride, "she is so very dear
to me that I scarcely like her to go out of my sight. I
want to have a talk with you, Percy, before you leave
for College, and lest I should have no other opportunity,
come to the library before you go to bed to-night, for I
have much to say."

Maud came down dressed for her ride, and very pretty
she looked in her bright blue riding habit, which set off
her slender form to great advantage, and well might Mr.
Earl gaze on her with love and pride in his glance. She
was indeed a girl to be proud of.

"Bless you, my darling," said he, as he kissed the sunny
face. " Have a nice ride, and take care of yourself. She
grows more like her mother every day," he murmured, as
she and Percy disappeared through the trees. " God
grant her life may be happier!"

The way to Norton was a favourite ride with Maud,
the road being nearly all the way bordered by dark pine
woods, and little frequented. On this particular day it
seemed more beautiful than ever. It was a ride that
Maud never forgot, and when her young heart was
bowed down with sorrow, the recollection of that happy
ride came back to her memory.

"How sad it seems, Percy, that I shall not see you

again for ever so long, because you are going to travel in your summer vacation, are you not?"

"Yes, Maud; uncle thinks it will be good for me, and I long to visit France and Germany. I shall not have time to get as far as 'la belle Italia,' but that I must leave for the present. By-the-bye, Maud, Reginald has started for Paris, has he not? If he is abroad when I go, I must look him up. I do not think I have seen him more than three or four times in my life, and until lately I did not even know of the existence of my cousin. Only fancy that, Maud! I don't think I shall mind if I never go back to that gloomy Lysle Castle. I declare I hate it, but I suppose I shall be obliged to stay there sometimes when I am of age."

Maud's commissions were soon executed, and the cousins on their return home, but the weather that had been so bright and beautiful in the morning, was now overcast, and a tremendous storm was evidently brewing.

"I fear, Maud, we shall not get home now before the rain," and as Percy spoke, the rain began to fall in large drops. "Where shall we go? Is there any shelter near, for we are going to have a fearful storm?"

"The only place I know of," said Maud, "is the old haunted house about a quarter of a mile from here."

"Well, let us get there as quickly as we can," said Percy.

Maud readily assented, and they started off at a gallop, and in a few minutes reached the haunted house. It was not a very inviting-looking place, but the storm had now come on in earnest, and any shelter was better than the open road.

"Why, what a strange place this is," said Percy, as they were standing under a portico that ran the whole length of the building, and afforded shelter to the cousins: "but suppose, Maud, I try the door, and see if we cannot find a better place to stay in until the storm ceases," saying which, Percy dismounted, and fastening his horse to one of the pillars that supported the portico, proceeded to try the door. The rusty lock readily gave way, and he entered a large hall with doors all round.

Seeing nothing very formidable, he opened one of them
and also one of the windows, which he calculated looked
out on to the portico, and having let in what little daylight he could, he discovered, to his surprise, that the
room was furnished, that there were even cinders in the
grate.

"This will be better for Maud than remaining out
there," and Percy went out to fetch her. Poor Maud
looked very pale and frightened, in spite of her effort
to appear brave in her cousin's eyes, but when Percy
came to take her into the house, she said in a frightened
tone of voice—

"Indeed I am very comfortable here ; see, very little
rain gets to me."

"Why, Maud," said Percy, "you surely don't mean to
say you are frightened ?"

After that Maud would not have hesitated to do anything, so getting off her horse, she allowed Percy to
escort her into the haunted house ; but when she saw
the dilapidated furniture and scene of desolation, her
courage nearly oozed away, and she would gladly have
been riding through the storm in preference to remaining, but she feared to risk her cousin's good opinion.

"Why, Maud, see here are the remains of a bouquet :
this house cannot have been shut up very long."

"Oh, yes, it was, some years before I was born."

"What is the story ?"

"Oh, please, dear Percy, don't mention it here."

Percy, like most very young men, laughed at anything
supernatural, and could not understand any one else not
doing the same, forgetting that very sensitive natures
are always nervous, and without being superstitious,
have a dread of nameless danger, although those very
natures would perhaps be as brave as lions in peril where
they could see the foe.

"Oh, Maud!" laughed Percy, "I declare you are
afraid of ghosts. What kind of a one is it that abides
on these premises ? Do tell me, for if there is one thing
more than another I have a fancy for, it is to see a
ghost. Come, tell me the story. Surely, Maud, you are

not afraid when I am here to protect you? It is a poor compliment you pay my prowess."

Maud, thus abjured, could not avoid complying.

"Well, then, Percy, I cannot vouch for the truth of it, because it all happened before I was born, but my maid, Lizzie, who told me the story, assured me her mother knew it to be true; but please, do not let Miss Meadowes know, for poor Lizzie might be scolded for telling me."

With this prelude, Maud related as follows:—

"About thirty years ago a Mr. Miller came from abroad with his wife, and took this house; it was a very old one, and had been empty some time, but his agent saw it, and liking its appearance, took it. The house had a bad reputation in the neighbourhood, but as the country people always attach a ghost to every house that is long unoccupied, it was not thought worth while to pay any attention to the report. Upholsterers and decorators were sent down, and the house was got ready to receive Mr. Miller and his wife. Expectation was at its highest pitch as to the antecedents of the new tenants of Manor House (for so it was called now). At last when everybody had almost given up expecting them, so long were they in making their appearance, a travelling carriage entered the village and went to the house; but though everybody tried with most laudable curiosity to gain information respecting the new comers, nothing was learnt. There were two servants at the house, and those were brought with the master, so nothing could be gleaned from that source; but the old woman, who had charge of the house until the arrival of the tenant, was besieged with inquiries. These she could only meet with one statement, that the two servants were evidently foreigners, and she thought brother and sister; as to Mr. Miller and his wife, she had seen nothing of them.

"Time passed, and although the servants were often seen in the village, nothing further was known about the affairs of the Manor House. Sometimes the villagers would meet on the least frequented roads, a dark, gloomy man, about thirty; but he always avoided them. There were many conflicting accounts, even as regarded his appearance and age; the only one thing they all agreed about being that there was evidently some mystery connected with him. At last, one night a visitor arrived at the Manor House, and a circumstance occurred which set all the village talking. About a week after the visitor's arrival, the news spread that something awful had happened at the House, and this reaching the ears of the magistrates, they sent two constables to inquire into the matter.

" When they arrived they found the House closed, and though they knocked and knocked, no answer could be got. At last they succeeded in forcing admission, and found the house empty.

" They went upstairs, and finding one of the doors locked, forced an entrance. It was a bedroom, fitted up with great luxury and taste, and, on approaching the bed, the curtains of which were drawn, they discovered the body of a lady. That she had been murdered there was no doubt, for there was a fearful wound in her side, and the bed-clothes were covered with blood. Who she was could not be known, but they saw that she was very beautiful, and looked calm and peaceful, as though asleep.

" Rewards were offered for the apprehension of Mr. Miller and the servants, but no clue could be obtained. Meanwhile the poor lady was buried, and the house shut up and left as it was; for no one would live there—not even to take care of it—after the fearful tragedy; and as people declared they saw the body walking round the house after dark, the road by it was gradually disused.

" At length about ten years after the murder, the sexton going into the churchyard early one morning, saw something lying on the poor lady's grave, and going up, found the body of a man quite dead. He called assistance, and had the body moved to the village inn. It was imagined that it was the body of Mr. Miller, and this was shown to be the case when the agent who took the house was telegraphed for, and came down : he immediately recognised the body ; and at the inquest, it transpired that the unhappy man had died from poison. The agent, a.

Mr. Carper, was examined, but could throw but little light on the fearful mystery. All he could tell was that he had been agent for years to the firm of Miller and Co.—a firm in the West Indies, and that he received advices from them to the effect that a young Mr. Miller, a nephew of one of the firm, was coming to reside in England, and would be looking out for a house in a retired part of the country, as Mr. Miller was in bad health and had a very great dislike to strangers. Mr. Carper had, thereupon, chosen the Manor House. Mr. Miller only called on him twice, and it struck him that he looked like a man suffering from some great physical or mental trouble. He knew little else, but upon making the most urgent enquiries, he had found that young Mr. Miller, for whom he had taken the Manor House, was personally unknown to the firm, and it was thought that some secret was connected with him ; but whatever it was, was never divulged. So ended the enquiry. Mr. Miller was buried by the side of the lady, and the Manor House was more shunned than ever.

" But the people had not quite done with the mystery, for about two years after the discovery of the body of the poisoned man, a woman came to the village inn. She was evidently a mulatto, and retained the traces of beauty in her advanced life, for she was not less than sixty years of age. She asked so many questions about the tragedy that people began to suspect, and one of the tradespeople remembered her as one of the servants Mr. Miller brought with him, and this being communicated to the magistrates, she was watched, and one night was seen going to this house. What she did here they did not know ; but after remaining about an hour, she left, and by some means finding she was under surveillance, managed to elude it and quitted the village, and although they searched far and wide, no trace of her could be discovered. However some time after this occurrence, letters came directed to Sir Tracy Johnson, the magistrate, who had been most active in trying to elucidate the mystery, and purporting to come from this woman, who was then dying in the Isle of France. Her story was a strange one, and cleared

5

up the mystery, as far as it ever can be cleared up, the principal actors being dead.

"The letter ran thus :—

"'I am dying, and dare not leave the world without telling the fearful secrets that have hitherto been locked in my own breast. I write to you because thousands of miles lie between us, and before you can take any steps against me I shall be far beyond your reach. Forty years ago I was young, beautiful and happy; but I had the misfortune to be born a slave, although the daughter of the proprietor of the plantation. My mother, a beautiful quadroon, died while I was almost a baby. My father never married, but made me his housekeeper. Time went on until I was seventeen, when he died intestate, and I was classed with his other property,—a slave ! Never shall I forget my feelings, I who had been reared in luxury and ease. All the good feelings of my heart turned to gall ; I cursed my father's memory, my mother and myself ; but curses were useless. The heir, Mr. Miller, took possession of the estate, and I was retained as a servant in the house of which I had been mistress. While I lived in this capacity, Mr. Miller grew enamoured of me, and soon began to show unmistakable signs that he regarded me with admiration. For my part, I was so friendless, that his kindness had quite won my heart, and I loved him with all the intensity of my mother's race. He could not marry me, he told me ; the law did not permit that, but he would give me his life's devotion in exchange for mine. I was poor and young, loving with all my heart, and for two years I experienced greater happiness than your cold northern natures can conceive of. At that time I began to fancy my master's love was decreasing, and although he always treated me and my child (for I had then a baby a few months old) with great tenderness, his absences from home were longer and more frequent, and at last the blow came—he was going to be married to a young lady, the daughter of a neighbouring planter ! At the news I nearly went mad. In my agony I almost determined to destroy myself and child, but at last recovered from a long illness, to find myself no longer in the beautiful room, to which I had grown accustomed, surrounded with everything that taste and money could buy, but in a plain whitewashed apartment, with only the common necessaries of life, and to hear that the master had brought home his new wife, and that I had been removed by his orders to the overseer's house, before his wife's arrival. What I felt I managed to conceal, for I had still my boy, and for his sake I felt that I would endure anything.

" 'In a few days my master came to see me, and said in a cold manner that he was glad I was better, and hoped I would do my best to gain the good opinion of my mistress, whose maid he promised I should become, and he left without one word to the boy, whom but a few months ago he used to caress and fondle, calling him his darling son, and lavishing every epithet of affection upon him.

" ' When he was gone, my heart was full to bursting, and I felt that very little more would turn me into a demon, but I strove to overcome my grief, and even then submitted for the sake of my worse than fatherless child. I found my new mistress a fair, insipid woman, with a cruel, mean nature. She hated me from the first, and in a short time complained that the care of my baby prevented my waiting on her as I ought, and that he must be taken away from me. I prayed on my knees, but in vain. He was removed, and in a short time died. Then, over his little corpse, I swore a fearful oath to be revenged on the whole of the murderers of my child; to live alone for vengeance, and devote my life to their destruction. I have fulfilled my oath. A child was born, the heir to all, and when I saw him fondled and loved, I thought of mine, dead through their cruelty, and renewed my oath. I could have killed the child, for I had the entire charge of it; but that did not satisfy me. I contemplated much more fearful vengeance. In a few years another boy was born. Now I began my work. The heir, whose name was George, loved me devotedly—far more than his own mother, and taking advantage of this I worked upon his feelings, instilling into his mind deadly hatred toward his young brother. Every childish fault I magnified into studied injustice to him, and succeeded at last in my designs. Mrs. Miller grew almost to fear her first-born, while she petted and humoured his brother, and George used to come to me for comfort. To me! whose every word instilled poison into his blood.

" ' So years rolled on, and the fearful quarrels between the brothers embittered the life of their father to such a degree, that he grew prematurely old. When George was twenty-five and his brother Edward twenty-two, a beautiful girl came as governess on the neighbouring plantation. It was said that a drop of black blood ran in her veins; I do not know if such was the case, but the suspicion was enough. Both Mr. and Mrs. Miller had the strongest hatred of this; but not so the sons. They both fell desperately in love with Olivia King, and I did my best to foster George's passion. The end of it was, that the lovers were secretly married, with my assistance, but Edward, loving as he did, soon found out the secret, and betrayed it to his father, whose rage was absolutely fearful. But as it was a thing not to be put aside, he made a provision for his elder son, on condition that he would go to live in England and never seek his father again.

" ' So the young couple left for England, taking me and a man who was a complete tool of mine, as their servants I had now Mr. George to myself, and I thought I had let my vengeance sleep long enough, so I began insinuating to my foster child, who was only too easy to be influenced, that the quietness and sadness of his wife was caused by her love for his brother. He was of a violent and jealous nature. I had laboured hard to increase these passions, and loving his wife as he did, his life was a perfect torture to him, while hers he made not much better. When we had been in England a short time, his brother Edward arrived one night, with a message from his father, who was ill, and wished to see his son before he died. Now was the time for a final

blow. I told George his brother had come to steal his
wife, and bade him see how she revived at the sight of
his rival. This drove him frantic, and in a fit of frenzy
he stabbed both his wife and brother. You found
Mrs. Miller, but Edward was not very far off; had you
searched the summer-house, you would have found
him.

" 'These deeds accomplished, I aided George to escape,
but on his voyage home in a sailing vessel, he went
mad. We arrived before the news could reach, and I
accompanied George to his father's, where he had to be
guarded, for he was dangerous. It was I who saw Mr.
Miller, and told the fearful story, exulting in my vengeance. As I unfolded it, he fell down in a fit, and
although he lived some months, never spoke again. At
last George, who had been under restraint, recovered his
reason, and nothing would do but he must return to the
scene of his crime (for he had loved his wife dearly,
although he had taken her life), and see her grave; the
rest you know.'

" And that was the end of the letter."

" Why, Maud, how clever you are to remember all
that," said Percy.

" Ah! I have heard the story so many, many times,
that I could not help remembering; but see Percy, it
has left off raining, and uncle will be dreadfully
frightened, and I shall be very glad to leave this fearful,
crime-stained house."

" Well, Maud, as you have been so good, we will go,
but you never told me if they found the brother's
body?"

" When we get away I will tell you, but not another
word in this house."

The cousins were soon in the saddle, and then Percy
reminded Maud of her promise.

" There is nothing to tell, except that after the old
woman's letter, they searched the summer-house, but
found nothing; so, whether the mulatto's story was true
or no, has never been discovered. But, Percy, how
eager you are to listen to such horrors; I shall think

you really believe in ghosts after this, in spite of your ridiculing them so."

"Ah, Maud, take care!" rejoined Percy; "you laugh now, but if you had seen your face in the haunted house, it was not quite such a rosy one, or what roses there were, were white ones. But there is the first dinner bell, and we have very nearly a mile to go. The wind must be this way for us to hear it so plainly. Don't be long dressing, Maud, or Uncle Walter will scold me for keeping his pet out so long," said Percy, as they drew up before the hall door.

Maud dismounted, and made such good use of her time, that she was down, and entered the dining-room as the soup was served. Mr. Earl and Percy were already there, and Maud had to undergo a great deal of teazing from Percy about their compulsory sojourn in the haunted house, but Mr. Earl came to the rescue, saying that Maud was a brave girl to go there at all, much more to stay above an hour in it.

"However, darling," he added, "I think it was better to stop there than to get wet."

But the recital of the adventure served to enliven the dinner hour. Maud felt very sad when she retired to the drawing-room (whither the gentlemen generally followed her very soon) to think that it was the last time Percy would be there. It seemed to her that she had known him all her life. Fortunately the gentlemen waited less time than usual before they entered the drawing-room, where Miss Meadowes sat at her knitting and Maud in one of the old-fashioned windows, making a pretence of reading, but in reality building castles in the air. Mr. Earl and Percy entered very softly, and Maud was in such a deep reverie that she did not hear them.

"What is my birdie reading," asked Mr. Earl, "to absorb her so?"

And stealing behind her, looked over her shoulder, and saw that the book was only open at the title-page.

"What! does my darling find the title of that book so charming that she cares to study it so long?"

Maud started up, blushing at being so caught.

"Ah, little one," said Mr. Earl, "the haunted house must have made a great impression. But Miss Meadowes has not heard the story, so I will relate it, while Percy here tries to amuse you and prevent your falling into another such study."

And so passed Percy's last evening at the Towers. At ten o'clock Maud and Miss Meadowes retired, leaving him alone with Mr. Earl.

"This room is dull, Percy, when Maudie goes," said the latter. "Come with me to the library; there is sure to be a fire there, and I want to talk with you."

The library was a large old-fashioned room, with oak furniture and crimson hangings; it had been given up to Mr. Earl's use since his return to the Towers. A bright fire burned on the hearth, for Mr. Earl liked warmth.

"Come, Percy, this looks comfortable; bring your chair near the fire. To-morrow you leave for college," said Mr. Earl, when they were comfortably seated "And in the summer vacation you propose travelling. Now, I have had a hard battle with Miss Lysle on your behalf; she thought you were in duty bound to spend the summer months with her at Lysle Castle; but I told her you wished to go to France and Germany, and I thought it right for you to do so, and guaranteed you would give me no cause to reproach myself for having consented to your wish. So you see, Percy, I am to be bail for your good conduct abroad, which you may be sure I should not have been had I not such entire confidence in you. On the other hand, you are young and heir to a very large fortune; many men will toady to you because of your wealth, but do not listen to bad advice, whatever you do wrong confess at once, and accept the punishment. Rest assured that by so doing you will escape much after misery. A fault never decreases by concealment. I have also another piece of advice, and that is—keep as clear as you can of Sir Reginald Clayton. Although dear Maud's half-brother, he is the last man I should like the son of my old and valued friend, Herbert Lysle, to choose as a companion. He is profligate and worthless, inheriting all the vices of his unfortunate race, and, for Maud's sake, look on his life with sadness ; he is the last of his line, and should he die the title will become extinct.'

"It is a strange family, is it not, Mr. Earl?" said Percy.

"Yes, a very strange one, Percy ; not one of the direct heirs ever died a natural death. Even Maud's father was not exempt from the rule ; when he married my sister, his son, Reginald, was a child five or six years old. His first wife, the mother of Reginald, was a distant relation of his, and his marriage with her had brought a great deal of property into the family. She died a year after her marriage, when Reginald was born. The young widower was very much shocked, but his heart was not much touched, for it had not been a marriage of love ; and when in a few years he married my sister, a life of happiness seemed before him, but he, alas! had the Clayton temper ; and, although he loved his wife devotedly. his violence helped to kill her. She was such a sweet, gentle creature, like Maud, who rejoices in the warm sunshine of tenderness and love, but to whom harshness and violence would be death ; and so it was with Lily. She soon drooped, and when Maud was quite a little one, she went to Heaven. Her husband grieved intensely ; indeed, after her death, he became an altered man, took no pleasure in either of his children, and one day when out shooting his gun went off and killed him on the spot. I was abroad at the time, but remember that the accident excited a great deal of attention, because it revived the old family story. But, Percy, you have led me into old family histories, when I only meant to give advice, and as it is getting so late, and you have to be up early to-morrow, we had better say good night, and God bless and protect you, my dear boy, for my dear old friend Herbert's sake."

And he wrung Percy's hand with fervent warmth.

Although Percy was up early the next morning he found his cousin down before him, ready to make his breakfast. "How good of you, Maud, to take this trouble," said he. " I thought when I said ' good bye' last night, that I should not have the pleasure of seeing you again, but this is delightful. It quite cheers one up, beside such kindness and attention is new to me. You know, Maud, you have quite spoilt me for Lysle Castle and Aunt Charlotte, so I think I shall be obliged to inflict my presence often on you during my vacation as a punishment."

Maud strove hard to be gay, but had great difficulty in sustaining her spirits, and at last, when her cousin bade her adieu, and she saw the carriage disappear among the trees, she could restrain her tears no longer, and retired to her room to indulge in the luxury of a really good cry.

" I have only known him a month, yet I love him as much as a brother ; more than Reginald," she exclaimed through her sobs.

The morning passed very slowly, so Maud made up her mind to visit little Charlie after luncheon. She reproached herself for her neglect of her little favourite, and determined to repair it as soon as possible. So luncheon being over, she set off, accompanied by her faithful Hero. As Maud entered Mrs, Morgan's cottage, she found the poor mother crying bitterly. " What is the matter?" said Maud.

" Oh ! Miss, Charlie is dying, I know, and my heart is breaking. "

" Nay, you must not let the child wake and see you suffering so, for his sake be calm." Saying this in a low voice, Maud advanced to the sofa where the child was, and when she saw the look of suffering on the little wasted face, she almost wished that Charlie might wake no more in this world. But as she gazed the eyes opened, and Charlie looked up with an enquiring expression. Maud was by his side in an instant, and was shocked to see how near the inevitable parting was. Charlie was too weak to speak, but he smiled in her face, and after a little time rallied, and broke silence by asking her to sing to him. Maud readily complied, although her heart felt too full for song, and presently she had the satisfaction of seeing the poor child drop off to sleep again. During that sleep the doctor arrived. He had not been to see his patient for some time, for although he knew that Charlie could never recover, he still thought he might live several years ; but now, when he saw him, he shook his head, and could not hide the conviction that the sands of life were running out fast, and that in all probability before night there would be one angel more in Paradise. Poor Mrs. Morgan, who had entered the room at the same time as the doctor, was convulsed with grief at these words, and, finding that she could not stifle her sobs, left the cottage to find her husband.

"Have you sufficient courage to remain, Miss Clayton?" asked the doctor, " a few hours is the utmost your little friend can last."

"Yes," said Maud, " I will remain with him unto the end."

Presently Morgan entered with his wife. He was a fine stalwart man, with a bold fearless look, but when his eyes rested on his sleeping child, so soon to pass away, his lip quivered, and the tears welled up in eyes unused to them, and only by a strong effort could he keep himself from sobbing outright. "Is there no hope, sir?" he asked.

" None."

" Oh, God, it is hard to say it, but Thy will be done." rejoined the wretched father, as he bent his head down on the table, his whole frame heaving with the violence of his emotion.

Not a sound was heard save the ticking of the clock and the smothered sobs of husband and wife for a long, long hour. Then Charlie awoke, and at once struggled to a sitting posture, a thing he had not accomplished for years, but the exertion was too much, and he fell back exhausted, with a sweet smile on his little wasted face. Maud bent down her ear, and caught one word, the last he spoke, as his soul winged its heavenward flight, and that word was " happy." As he uttered it a change passed across the little face, there was a slight convulsive shudder, and he was gone.

CHAPTER IX.

COVERS FOR SIX.

NEARLY two years have elapsed since the events related in the last chapter. It is again the month of November, but the weather is brighter and more cheerful than on the evening on which we first introduced the reader to our heroine. Two young men are standing together on the steps of one of the fashionable clubs in St. James's Street.

"I say, Lysle, are you going to see this new actress to-night? The papers puff her finely," said the elder of the two, a dissipated looking man, with a drawling voice.

"Don't know. What is her name?"

"Wilmot or Wilton, something of the kind, but I always forget names, it is such a bore to remember them. But do come, old fellow, several of the men are going, for Sir Archibald says she is a perfect beauty."

"All right. But there is Clayton coming across. See you again at dinner," said Percy, as he ran down the steps to meet Sir Reginald.

Percy Lysle is very much altered since we saw him last, he is a very handsome young man, far better looking than he gave promise to be; but he has a worn haggard look, that tells of late hours and champagne suppers in not very reputable company. Sir Reginald is much the same. In the two years that have passed there has been but little change, except that he looks more sardonic and restless than ever. Percy seems very glad to see him, and presses his hand eagerly.

"Why, Reginald, when did you come back? I thought that you were to be away a month at least."

"Oh, no; nothing doing, and I cannot endure those shooting parties. After a week found it awfully slow, so made Adolphe pack up my traps, and here I am."

" But how did you leave Maud ?"

" Not very well ; she is coming up to town in a week
or two, and then, old fellow, you must settle down. I
thought her little ladyship seemed rather disappointed at
your not coming down with me, although she said nothing.
How pretty she is! By Jove, Percy, you are a lucky
fellow to gain her without any trouble. In her first
season too ; but I must say for one so near matrimony
you are uncommonly cool, and if I did not know better,
should say indifferent ; but after next week you will
have to alter, so I suppose I must not find fault. But
what are you going to do to-night ?"

" Oh, Ellis wants me to go and see some new actress
who has made a hit. Will you come ?"

" Yes, I may as well."

" Then come and dine with me, Ellis and a few of our
fellows are coming."

Percy was now in a crack regiment, noted for its
follies and extravagances, and these " fellows" were his
brother officers. The dinner passed off as most of those
affairs do, with a great many jokes uttered, and a great
deal of wine drank. After eight o'clock Percy Lysle
entered the large stage box of the theatre, accompanied
by his friends.

The piece they were going to see was a new one,
written expressly for the new actress, and was the story
of a peasant maid loved by the lord of the village, and
then deserted, and driven to revenge on her betrayer.
As the curtain rises, the new favourite enters, amid loud
applause. What is it that makes Sir Reginald pause in
the midst of a story he is telling Ellis ? and why does
Percy Lysle change colour ? Because the former recog-
nises in the new actress the woman he has been seeking
for two years, whose image he has in vain striven to
banish from his mind, and the latter again sees his ideal
of female beauty. Yes, the *debutante* is Cora. The two
years have only changed her from a lovely child into a
glorious woman. The first act passes over, Sir Reginald
sits back as one under a spell ; the second act commences,
but Cora is no longer the love-sick village girl, she is

now the woman, with a heart full of revenge towards the man who has betrayed her. Well may Sir Reginald turn pale as she reproaches her lover for his perfidy, his memory carrying him back to the time when words like those were spoken to him, and the dim spectres of the past bring anything but pleasure to his restless feelings.

"Who wrote that piece?" he said, as the curtain fell for the second time.

"I do not know, but how wonderfully acted," said Percy, "and what a lovely creature!"

All further remarks were put an end to by the ensuing and final act. In this one the acting was superb, and when at last Cora stabbed herself, Sir Reginald could stand it no longer, but left his box. Then Cora was called before the curtain, and received an ovation from her audience. Percy was in a perfect fever of excitement, and the image of poor Maud faded before the presence of this golden-haired siren. He did not care to stay for the afterpiece, in which Cora did not play; so bidding his companions good night, left them abruptly.

Outside the theatre he encountered Sir Reginald, who was walking up and down, evidently waiting for some one.

"Why, Reginald, how was it you left before the end of the piece?"

"Because the place was so confoundedly hot, and I did not feel very well. But what do you think of this new actress?"

"Oh, she is splendid, glorious! I never saw a lovelier or more enchanting creature," cried Percy, with enthusiasm.

"Take care! That is not the way a man should talk who is engaged to be married to my sister," and a sneer passed over Sir Reginald's features as he spoke. "It is lucky for you that the peerless Maud does not hear your rhapsodies."

The expression more than the words recalled Percy to himself, and muttering some apology, he would have excused himself from accompanying Sir Reginald; but he would take no denial, and insisted on Percy going to

supper with him, as had been agreed before they went to
the theatre. Nothing more was said until Sir Reginald's
chambers were reached, where there were covers laid for
six. Percy looked in astonishment, for he had no idea
that his cousin expected any visitors, and wondered who
the other four would be. He was not, however, kept
long in suspense ; for a loud knock proclaimed an arrival,
and two gentlemen entered together. They were evidently perfectly at home, and greeted Sir Reginald with
great familiarity.

" Allow me to present my cousin, Mr. Lysle, to you,
Count de Bourg and Marquis de Bournville, old friends
of mine, Percy."

Percy bowed; he did not much like the looks of the
Count or Marquis either ; but before he could quite
decide in his own mind what there was about them that
he disliked, the other two guests arrived, and supper was
served. The new arrivals were introduced as Major
Green and Captain Lance. They all seemed well acquainted, and Percy was the only stranger. For the first
time since his acquaintance with his cousin, Mr. Earl's
warning flashed across his mind ; he had heard men speak
mysteriously of the strange society Sir Reginald kept,
and the high play that went on in his rooms, but had never
seen either the one nor the other, and felt to-night he
was to be initiated into both. He did not quite like the
faces of Sir Reginald and his guests. He was one of
those who feel instinctive likes or dislikes at first sight,
and certainly the men at supper were not calculated to
inspire confidence or esteem. The Count de Bourg was
a tall dark man, about forty, with a sardonic cast of
countenance, and smooth, tiger-like manners. He had a
beautiful set of teeth, of which he seemed very vain,
smiling often on purpose to show them. His friend, the
Marquis de Bournville, had no particular traits : he was
fair and commonplace, except for an eager, cunning look
in his eyes, that resembled a fox's. Major Green, who
was an Irishman, with a broad brogue, and a reckless,
devil-may-care air, seemed much more like a free lance
than a soldier in her Majesty's service. Captain Lance

was the opposite of them all; and yet the Count's tiger-like smile, the Marquis's cunning .eyes, and the Major's reckless air, did not inspire Percy with half so much distrust as Captain Lance's good looks. Yet it was a face born to charm, with its dangerous fascination. Rather above the middle height, he had the figure and form of an Apollo, golden curls clustering round a forehead of marble whiteness, bright blue eyes lit up features cast in a perfect mould. What then could there be in him to inspire mistrust and dread? Yet so it was. Perhaps, if you looked closely, you would see that the lips were a trifle too thin, and that the white teeth were unpleasantly pointed, like those of a wild animal. The blue eyes also were more like steel in colour, and seemed to burn with the brightness of their glances. But the hands told more tales than anything else. They were long, white and supple, with winding fingers, reminding one disagreeably of what would be their deadly strength if clasped round one's throat. They were the hands that might have belonged to Cæsar Borgia. It is a fact that the hand, more than any other part of the human frame, indicates truly the character of the individual, and opinions on character based on them nearly always turn out correct.

Percy caught himself often gazing intently at the Captain's white hand, thinking how cruel it looked in spite of its delicate colour; and had he known the gallant Captain's real nature, he would not have wondered at the repugnance he inspired, or the shudder which passed through his frame when that white hand closed round his own.

Few knew much of Algernon Lance's life; but what was known was so little to his credit, that even the fastest men fought shy of his society.

The supper was perfect, and under its exhilarating influence Percy began to find his first impressions of his new acquaintances assuming a brighter hue. The Count told charming little stories, and if their moral was not always first-rate, they caused a great deal of laughter and amusement. The Major was not behindhand, and Cap-

tain Lance had such quiet, gentlemanly manners, and
such brilliant sarcasm played over his conversation, that
before supper ended Percy had quite forgotten his first
impressions of him, and had arrived at the conclusion
that he was a most charming man, quite unlike any one
he had ever before seen.

"Well, gentlemen," said Sir Reginald, "what do you
say to a rubber?"

"With all my heart," replied each of the others.

And if for a moment Percy's former suspicion crossed
his mind, he dismissed it immediately. The gentlemen
retired to Sir Reginald's card-room; for so attached was
he to that pastime, that he had a room at his chambers
fitted up on purpose.

"Why not have some game at hazard? It's three
times the fun," said Major Green.

"With all my heart," said Sir Reginald, "if all are
willing. You will join us, Lysle?"

"Oh! with pleasure," replied Percy, forgetting a promise not to touch cards that he had given Maud.

"Then Lance will be your opponent, and you, Marquis,
take the Major, and you, Count, give me my revenge for
the last evening we spent together."

The morning dawned, and still found them playing;
and when at last the party broke up, Percy was a
winner to the amount of several hundreds. The passion
engendered by his success had already began to work, so
that when Captain Lance, who bore his losses with perfect equanimity, proposed that they should meet the following night at his rooms, Percy accepted without the
slightest hesitation. It was broad daylight before Percy
reached his rooms, in Albermarle-street, and not feeling
particularly bright himself, after his night of excitement,
retired to bed at once. When he rose, late in the afternoon, he felt some compunction for his broken promise
to Maud, but remembered he had given his word to meet
his new friends again that night. He argued with himself
that it would be impossible to keep his promise; "besides,"
said he to himself, "she had no right to exact such a
promise from me. Every fellow plays, and I should
appear a milksop in their eyes by refusing."

Percy Lysle was very young, or such flimsy consi-
derations would have had no weight with him; but he
was one of those who could only learn the lesson of life
by hard experience. It has been intimated that Percy
fancied himself in love with his pretty cousin, Maud,
who had already gained the reputation of a beauty. On
seeing her so much admired and sought after, he had
before the end of her first season proposed for her hand,
and had been accepted: but, alas! for the prospect of
sweet Maud's happiness, it was not her image that
occupied his thought exclusively as he walked down to his
club.

"Where did you go last night, Lysle?" said Ellis, as
he entered. "Could not find you anywhere when we
came out."

"I went with Clayton home to his rooms to supper, and
we had a jolly night of it, two or three capital fellows."

"Indeed! who were they? Any of our set?"

"No; they were all strangers to me, two foreigners,
a Major Green, and the other an awfully nice fellow,
named Lance."

"Whew!" cried Ellis, taking his cigar from his mouth
and staring at Percy; "take my advice, Lysle, and
keep clear of him. I am no saint, but I should hesitate
before I associated with such a man as Algernon Lance;
he is devoid of honour, truth, and feeling, and the ruin
of many an unfortunate man can be laid at his door,—
keep clear of that devil as you value your honour."

Percy gazed in amazement. Could this earnest man
be the drawling exquisite he had always thought him?
Before he could express his astonishment, Ellis had
resumed his cigar and relapsed into his usual listless
manner.

"Who is this Lance, then, and what has he done?"
asked Percy.

"Well, old fellow, you will soon find out; but if you
want more information on the subject, go to young Dixon,
or Major Gask; they do say that Lance dare not meet
them: no one knows why, but it must be something very
bad, for I only once heard his name mentioned before

G

the Major, but he turned perfectly livid, and the expression
of hate that passed over his face haunted me for days."

"But the Major is so reserved," said Percy; "no one
dare ask him anything."

"Well, then, ask Lance how he likes the Major when
you see him, and mention that you are a most particular
friend of his, and see how he takes it; but good bye, I
am leaving town for a few days. Shall see you, I suppose,
when I come back."

Percy dined alone, with his thoughts for companions;
but they were not of the pleasantest. Do what he would
he could not divest himself of the idea that he had
forfeited his honour as a gentleman in breaking the
promise made to Maud, and then again was he not
behaving most disloyally towards her whose heart he
had won, by allowing his thoughts to stray from her to
the young actress, who had made so great an impression
on him? She who was so good and pure; how her heart
would ache, did she know how fast he was losing all title
to her respect and affection. Nevertheless, Percy went
again that night to the theatre where Cora performed.
He felt a passionate admiration for her, (he could scarcely
call it love); but it was quite unlike the calm affection
he entertained for his cousin. During the evening the
opposite box attracted his attention, for it was evidently
let, and yet he had seen no one in it. So, sitting back,
he began to watch, and presently saw Sir Reginald, with
Algernon Lance, enter the box. A sharp pain darted
through Percy's heart, as he saw the intense gaze of his
cousin fixed upon Cora; but how much worse it became
when he saw her recognise Sir Reginald and seem about
to fall upon the stage. Now he hated his cousin. He
could have killed him, and yet he was engaged to be
married to his sister, a sweet girl, who loved him truly
and devotedly. Alas! for poor Cora, it was her misfortune to inspire mad absorbing passions in the hearts
of men; her beauty intoxicated them, making them forget
even honour for her sake.

Sir Reginald saw her recognition of him and drew
hope from it; but he would not have felt so happy had

he known that all love for him had died out of her heart
long ago, and that the cause of her emotion at the sight
of him was fear and vexation,—fear, knowing how he
had tracked her, and vexation that she could not control
herself enough to appear calm and undisturbed. And
how Percy's heart would have throbbed with pleasure,
instead of pain, could he have been told that he had
been recognised as the youth with the bouquet of her
first appearance. Everything connected with that night
would ever be remembered by Cora, and Percy's brown eyes
among the number. But, as we cannot see into the
hearts of others, Sir Reginald felt triumphant and Percy
miserable and unhappy. He sat back in his box and
watched Sir Reginald, and when, at the end of the piece,
he saw him hurriedly leave his box, he did likewise, and
followed him round to the stage-door. It was true, then.
His worst suppositions were correct; his cousin knew
this actress. His brain was in a whirl. Maud, honour,
everything was forgotten, even the discreditable fact
that he had condescended to play the spy on Sir
Reginald. How he despised himself, and yet this mad
infatuation was hurrying him on against his better
nature. Hidden in a doorway, he became a witness of
the meeting of Cora with his cousin; but he could not
hear what was said. They walked too far away, but he
saw Sir Reginald hand Cora into her carriage, and heard
the word, "to-morrow."

How he got to Lance's rooms in the Albany, Percy
scarcely knew, but when he arrived there, he found himself
the first, and had time to guess at the character of his
host by his surroundings. That he was fond of luxury
and self indulgence was clear from the splendour and
elegance of his rooms, quite unlike those usually occupied by bachelors. The room Percy was now in was
evidently a drawing-room, with its hangings of blue silk,
and furniture to match. Exquisite pictures of lovely
girls hung on the walls, and the air was laden with the
perfume of costly flowers. In a few minutes Lance and
Clayton entered, apologising for keeping him, but pleading as an excuse a visit to an old friend who had detained

6—2

them. How Percy despised them for their falsehood, and yet he was acting one far more despicable! The arrival of Major Green and the rest of the party of the previous night prevented any reply, and the guests having assembled, supper was announced. Lance led the way to the supper-room. Everything that art and ingenuity could invent for ease and comfort adorned this room, and the supper was a miracle of daintiness. But in spite of all Percy felt ill at ease. He drank deeply, but could not shake off the feeling of oppression, and was glad when supper ended and cards were proposed, thinking that the excitement of the card-table might dispel the ennui that hung over him.

"You must give me my revenge, Lysle," said Lance.

And Percy in a very short time found his pockets lighter by a few hundreds; luck had turned against him.

"What, Percy, has the fickle jade deserted you?" said Sir Reginald. "I have a confounded headache, so am going, but do not let me disturb you."

"Stay, Reginald, I will go with you, for it is very late, and I do not care to play any more to-night."

A shade of vexation passed over Lance's face, but he repressed it so instantaneously that Percy thought he must have been mistaken, especially, when at parting, Lance shook him cordially by the hand, and renewed his invitation to visit him again.

"How do you like Lance?" asked Sir Reginald, in a careless tone, when he and Lysle found themselves strolling towards Albormarle Street, for he had volunteered to accompany Percy, saying that a walk would do his head good.

"I hardly know; he is awfully handsome and jolly— all that sort of thing, but there is something about him that I cannot make out."

"Is there?" said Sir Reginald. "I never noticed anything peculiar, and I have known him for many years."

"He must be very rich to live in the style he does. Is he an elder or only son?"

"Upon my word, Percy, I do not know; I never in-

quired about his family or means ; he pleased me, and
that is all I care for in an acquaintance. He has lived
abroad several years, for, although he looks such a boy,
he is over thirty. I have never asked him questions
concerning his life before I knew him, and I should
advise you not to try it either, for he is rather a fiery
one when put out. However, one meets a jolly set of
men at his rooms, so what does it really matter who or
what he is? But here you are, at home, old boy, so
good night."

And Sir Reginald sauntered away, and Percy retired
to bed to dream that he was talking to the beautiful
actress, and that all of a sudden Algernon Lance tore him
away, and dragged him down, all his efforts to escape
being fruitless, till at last he became unconscious.

But let us leave Percy to sleep off his excitement, and
return to the rooms he has just left. The whole of the
guests have departed, and Algernon Lance is alone in
the supper-room, which is now clear. He sits gazing
into the now expiring fire, then starting up, begins
pacing the room. Judging from the restless, perturbed
expression of his face, his thoughts are far from agreeable. At last he stops his wild striding to and fro, looks
around him, and laughs a forced, discordant laugh, full
of bitterness.

"What a fool I am," he ejaculates; "the dead can
not revisit the earth, and yet his words sing in my ears.
Pshaw! it's all old women's stories, but for all that a
glass of brandy will do me no harm," and going to the
sideboard, he poured some out, and drank it off eagerly.
"Ah! that is better. Now for my winnings—five hundred and fifty—not bad; but if Clayton had not taken
the fool away, I should have been richer by a cool
thousand. But better luck next time. Nearly five,"
he continued, looking at his gold repeater. "I shall not
go to bed now ; what is the use? Besides, directly I
lie down, that thing comes," and the man shuddered
fearfully, glancing around him, and resumed his seat,
but only to start up again and walk the room till he was
thoroughly exhausted.

To look at him now, Percy would not have wondered at his dread. The face was still that of an angel, but a fallen one—the impersonation of Lucifer, after his fall. The golden curls seemed to writhe and twist like serpents, the eyes flashed like burning steel, and the thin lips drawn back disclosed the white, pointed teeth, gleaming brightly. All tended to inspire fear. A face that was indeed beautiful, but deadly as a serpent's. The hands clasped and unclasped with a strange, spasmodic action, and he seemed unlike anything human.

Algernon Lance was a man without a soul, if we can imagine such a being. His wickedness had not developed itself until he had nearly reached man's estate. That bright head had been kissed and fondled by a loving mother in infancy, little dreaming that she had brought into the world a monster, but luckily for her she did not live to see, and died in happy ignorance. No one re-deeming quality existed in his character. Base, cruel, self-indulgent, and ferocious, he united the craft of the serpent with the bloodthirstiness of the panther, and the brutality alone found in man when thoroughly de-based. And yet he was not a coward; he would never shrink from personal danger, but it was not the courage of a true man. With the ability of one almost without a soul, he seemed possessed by the spirit of evil, yet this man was superstitious, and feared what he professed to disbelieve in—viz., beings of another world. And truly if ever any one was haunted, it was he. Perhaps the phantoms were the creation of his own conscience, but from whatever cause, he could never endure to be alone at night.

And well might he be haunted by fearful dreams, for those hands, the indications of his character, were stained with the blood of a fellow-creature. Nor was the taking of a life his only crime. How many an unfortu-nate woman had he through her most tender virtues, love and truthfulness, hurled from her pedestal of purity, to herd with the abandoned of her sex, deserted and forgotten, to fall at last into a pauper grave, or rush headlong into eternity, by a suicidal hand!

Such was the sworn friend of Sir Reginald Clayton, and bidding fair to hold the same position with Percy Lysle, unless some good angel whispered in his ear a timely warning. To do Sir Reginald justice, he had no idea of the true character of his associate, for had he known that murder had dyed the hand he clasped in friendship, he would have thrown it from him, as though it had been an adder.

The morning light struggled into the apartment where Algernon Lance was pacing to and fro, and with a sigh of relief he opened the window, as though to welcome it, and then proceeded to ring the bell.

In answer to the summons, a gentle, middle-aged domestic appeared, one of most respectable mien, such as one would scarcely expect to see in Lance's employ ; but men said that the servant, in spite of his appearance, was a fitting attendant for such a master. Joe White's history was a strange one. Left an orphan very young, he managed to get into training stables as a help to the stable boys, and in time became exalted to the position of stable boy, but being found out in some very unfair conduct was discharged. He then knocked about London for some time, eking out a miserable existence by holding horses, running errands, and so forth, and having occasionally helped the servants belonging to an eccentric old gentleman, he was eventually taken into his service. But one day White and the lady's maid were missing, and with them a large quantity of plate and jewellery. They were tracked, discovered, and convicted —the woman getting three months' imprisonment and the man six. When his time expired he came out a ruffian as well as thief, for his punishment, so far from doing him good and teaching him better, threw him into the society of men far worse than himself, men who boasted of their crimes. He had kept up a correspondence with the unfortunate lady's maid, who, without character or friends, had no one to cling to but himself, so when he came out of prison he went to her lodgings in Holborn. But better for her, poor wretch, had she died before she renewed his acquaintance. He was now the associate of burglars and thieves, and she, who had been respectably brought up in a country village, far away, suffered persistent cruelty, before she could mingle with his chosen friends. His respectable appearance made him of great use to his companions, as he served the purpose of decoy better on that account. In spite of his brutality and cunning he was a coward, and kept out of all exploits likely to bring him into personal danger, but he got into trouble, nevertheless. The poor woman he had ruined led a fearful life, and at last died from the effects of his blows. He was again taken, this time for murder. There being no evidence to convict him, he was discharged, but not a better although a wiser man, for he to all appearance quietly eschewed his former companions, but baffled all the efforts of the police to find out by what means he lived. At last a dreadful tragedy occurred; a jeweller's shop was broken into, and property to a large amount stolen; the porter, who happened to sleep on the premises, hearing the noise, disturbed the burglars, and was found brutally murdered. Large rewards were offered for the apprehension of the perpetrators of this outrage, but without avail. Information reached the jeweller that if the reward were increased he might hear of something; it was accordingly done, and in a few days Joe White informed against three men. Through his evidence two of them were condemned to transportation for twenty-one years, and the other was hanged. As he received the reward one of the men, as he was leaving the dock, bade him beware, for when he returned he would have his life. But twenty-one years was a long time to look forward to, so Joe White thought and felt secure, but he did not dare return to his previous home, so with his five hundred pounds, the price of blood, he bade adieu to the great city. How Algernon Lance became acquainted with him, or where he met him, no one knew, and so many years had elapsed since his disappearance, that no one could possibly recognise in the quiet, respectable middle-aged servant the man who was held up to public execration for betraying his companions for the very crime he himself planned and helped to execute.

But though the public had forgotten all about him, Joo had an unpleasant feeling that one who had reason to remember him, who was not likely to forget to pay back the debt with interest, would in spite of time and all disguise recognise him, should he ever come across his path, and as the years rolled by and it got nearer to the appointed time, he grew more and more apprehensive, until life became a burden to him, so much terror did the thought raise in his imagination. His nature was too utterly callous to feel remorse for his crimes, but no remorse could rack his craven heart like the certainty that there was one man who, if living (and he felt sure he was), would hunt him down mercilessly in spite of everything.

"Did you ring, sir?" said he to Lance, as he stood with the door in his hand.

"Of course I did ring. Bring me some breakfast directly."

The man disappeared, but soon returned, bringing a tray furnished with everything likely to tempt the appetite of a man who had been indulging in a night of dissipation. But delicacies tempted in vain, Algernon Lance had no appetite, and retired to his bedroom to snatch, if possible, a few hours' sleep.

CHAPTER X.

LOVE AND HATE.

IN a room neatly, but elegantly furnished, in a house at the West End, sat Cora. She had a book in her hand, but she was not reading. The clock on the mantelpiece striking two, roused her from her reverie, and at the same moment Sir Reginald was announced. As he entered, Cora drew herself up, and bowed in a stately manner. It was not quite the reception he expected, and induced a little embarrassment, which increased when, in a cold careless voice, as though she addressed the verieststranger, Cora enquired, "To what was she indebted for the honour of Sir Reginald's visit?"

For a moment he was unable to reply, but soon gained confidence, thinking it impossible she could have ceased to care for him.

"Cora, can you ask the reason of my visit? Do you not know that I love you, and that for the pleasure of seeing you I would travel a thousand miles, and for one smile would gladly sacrifice my life? Besides, last night, did you not give me permission to visit you? You loved me once, you cannot have forgotten me so soon—scarcely two years ago. I have searched unceasingly since the time we parted, but without avail, and little did I think when I heard of the actress who had turned the heads of half the men in town by her beauty and talent that it was the woman for whom I had so long sought. I did wrong you once, but forgive me, and be my wife, Cora, you will never be loved again as I love you. Give me some hope?"

And Sir Reginald in his excitement seized Cora's hand, but it was only for a moment, for the next instant Cora had snatched it from his grasp, and stood before him with flashing eyes.

"So, Sir Reginald, you would make me your wife? Remember your own words, 'Marriage is the grave of love.' Do you not still believe in that noble sentiment? Consent to marry you!" said Cora, with biting sarcasm. "Never, never! But listen to me, Sir Reginald, I loved you once, I will not deny it; I loved you with all a young girl's first true innocent love. How did you repay it? By seeking to make me the most degraded of my sex. You won my heart only to crush it by your baseness. You would have repaid my devotion by plunging me into a life of infamy, and after a time deserting and leaving me. But the God you outraged gave me strength to resist temptation, and I fled from it with no greater sorrow than a bruised heart. Now you would make me your wife; do you remember my words at that last meeting? I have not forgotten them, if you have, and my sentiments are still the same. I would not marry you to save my life. I despise you, and your name causes me no emotion save those of pity and contempt."

Sir Reginald's heart had been a prey to conflicting emotions, love, hate, and revenge, during the time Cora was speaking, and now he felt he could have killed her where she stood, but stifling his passions, he turned on Cora a look of diabolical hate, which haunted her for many a long day.

" That is your final decision, is it ? Now listen to me. I will have a brave revenge for what you have said to me. I retract my offer of marriage, but you shall sue at my terms for it, and I will treat your prayer as you have treated mine. You have made a deadly enemy of one who would have given his life for you, and turned his love—a love such as you can never dream of—into the blackest hate. You shall be mine, I swear it, but not on the terms I offered you just now ; I will make you the laugh and scoff of the town. So, sweet mistress Cora, beware, and farewell, until we meet again."

With a fiendish laugh, Sir Reginald left the room. Poor Cora was so frightened and bewildered that she could scarcely refrain from weeping, but the consciousness of having done her duty restrained her tears. " Besides," thought the brave girl, " why should I fear? The power that saved me from destruction two years ago will watch over me and protect me from the machinations of that wicked man."

Cora had risen in her profession since we last saw her. It was the result of her talent, and the good fortune that befel her in being seen by a London manager in a part that suited her. He happened to be looking out for beauty and talent, and being struck with Cora, engaged her. The interval between the time of the engagement and that of her appearance in town, she employed in the provinces, gaining practice and a greater knowledge of stage business, without which, no matter how great may be the genius of the actress, it is impossible for her to succeed.

A piece was written to suit her peculiar talent, and Cora's beauty and grace crowned both herself and the author with immediate success, and she awoke in the morning to find herself famous.

The delight it caused to the fond parents to see their child so admired and respected, gave Cora almost a more lively feeling of pleasure than the success itself, and that was very great; for it was so new to her, and the adulation she received so intoxicated her, that at the time she would not have renounced her profession to be made a princess. Nothing would have persuaded her that she would ever cease to care for the perilous position of a public favourite, and sigh for a life of peace and love, far away from the noise and tinsel glitter of the theatre.

"Why, Cora, what is the matter?" said Mrs. Wilton, quite altered from the querulous invalid we saw two years ago, now looking strong and happy, thanks to her daughter's prosperity. "What ails my darling? and who was that dark, evil-looking man, who just now left?"

Cora would have given the world to have been able to throw herself into her mother's arms, and pour out her fears and sorrows on her loving heart; but she dared not, for then she would have had to confess the deceit she practised two years before, and she had not courage to do that; so she made an excuse that the gentleman in question having seen and admired her at the theatre, finding out where she lived, had called, but would never do so again. Mrs. Wilton looked grave, for she did not approve of strangers presuming to call on her pretty daughter.

"You must not see anyone that calls, Cora, without I am present, in future," said she; and Cora saw she was vexed, and strove to change the subject, but it was some time before she could succeed in chasing the cloud from her mother's brow.

Hardly had she succeeded, when they were interrupted by a double knock.

"Who can it be, I wonder? But no matter; I am here to receive them," said Mrs. Wilton, putting on her sternest frown.

But there was no occasion this time, for the visitor was none other than our friend Ella. Cora gave a cry of delight at the sight of her friend, and Mrs. Wilton, who, although she did not know much of Ella personally, had heard of her good conduct and devotion to her mother, welcomed her cordially.

"When did you come to town, dear?" asked Cora; for Ella had been playing in the provinces since we last saw her, not having met with Cora's good fortune.

"Only the day before yesterday. We closed at Muggleton last Saturday; been doing splendid business, and my benefit was tremendous,—not a box unlet. But what a star you have become! I read such a notice of you, and you don't know, darling, how pleased I was to see it; for I am sure you deserve it."

This compliment to her child quite won Mrs. Wilton's heart, and she prevailed on Ella to stay and accompany them to the theatre to see Cora play.

"But I can only see the first piece, dear," said Ella, "for poor mamma is very ill, and Eunice must not stay up so very late."

Left alone, the two friends had much to talk over.

"How well you are looking, Cora, and how tall you are growing. Do you know I thought you would be short; but you are nearly as tall as I am."

"I declare, Ella," said Cora, "you have grown thinner and paler. There is some secret. I have it: you are in love!"

Ella smiled, but such a wintry smile that Cora felt sure that her old friend was unhappy; but knowing her reserved nature, refrained from pressing her for an answer, and changed the subject.

"Do you know, Ella," she said, "I saw Rose; I do not remember her other name, but you know who I mean. She was in the *ballet* at Drury Lane, and she told me that you had paid back all the money they lent you when you sprained your foot, and had given them a present besides. She looked very shabby, and I asked her if she was out of an engagement. She said 'No,' but from her hesitating manner I think she is only at one of the minor theatres."

"Ah, Cora! what changes have occurred in the two years. Do you remember a girl called Kate?"

"Yes, indeed, I do ;" and Cora called to mind a certain night when a ring was brought to her, and Kate advised her to accept it.

"Well, that girl left the *ballet* to live with some gentleman named Lance. She broke her mother's heart by doing so, and of course he deserted her, leaving her to starve, and she ended her career by jumping into the river. She was a giddy girl, but I cannot help pitying her, poor creature! for, after all, she was very kind-hearted, and if I had known she was in want she should not have been driven to such a fearful end, while I had a shilling in my pocket. But I am making you cry, Cora. I do not know what has come to me to-day ; but now for the cheerful side. You know that Ellen Morris has married, and left the stage. I saw her the other day, looking very happy, and she has quite a patronising way with her now, and evidently thinks her husband the most wonderful man in the world. She asked me to go home with her, which I did. She has a very pretty house ; old Mrs. Morris is installed there in comfort. Everything was good, but rather gaudy, and Ellen herself too fussy for my idea of good breeding ; but still she is very happy and makes a capital wife. Her husband, who is a stock-broker, is twenty years older than herself ; but that suits Ellen, who was always a matter-of-fact girl, without a grain of romance in her composition. However that staid, respectable, middle-aged gentleman made up his mind to marry a *ballet* girl is beyond my comprehension ; but the blind god plays strange pranks."

Little more passed before it was time to go to the theatre. Mrs. Wilton always accompanied her daughter and helped her dress, but this night she was going to ask permission to be allowed a box with Ella, to see Cora act. The house was full, as usual, and Cora was received with the same enthusiasm.

"See, uncle, there is the pretty girl we saw at Elverton two years ago," cried a clear, ringing voice, which could be none other but sweet Maud Clayton's, and hers it was. But the two years had passed lightly over her, save that she was lovelier, if possible, than when we saw her last, and more fragile and delicate looking. "Look, uncle, there is Percy," Maud added, suddenly, and her cheeks, before so pale, flushed a rosy red. "How surprised he will be to see us."

Mr. Earl looked, and a frown passed over his face as he noticed Percy's evident admiration for Cora; but presently his face became deadly pale, and he clutched the back of his chair as Algernon Lance entered Percy's box.

"Excuse me, Maud, darling, for a moment," said he, as he got up. "I have just seen a person I have not met for years, and must go, but will be back again shortly."

Going into the refreshment room, he wrote a few words on his card, and sent the box keeper with it to Percy Lysle. He had no cause to describe him to the man, for Percy was too well known, and Mr. Earl felt sick at heart, at the knowledge of the life Percy was leading, and the company he kept. Percy made his appearance directly, and looked very confused and guilty, when he saw Mr. Earl's stern face.

"So, Percy Lysle, this is the life you lead," said Mr. Earl. "You who are engaged to my niece. You cannot come down to visit her, who is soon to be your wife, because you are unwell; but you can frequent a theatre every night, and keep the society of a villain. Thank God, my old friend Herbert Lysle never lived to see his only son a companion of the greatest scamp and scoundrel in London." And Mr. Earl turned away, overcome by the violence of his emotion.

"Sir, Mr. Earl, hear me," said Percy. "That I have been weak, wicked, and ungrateful, I do not deny, but, believe me, I knew nothing of the character of the man you speak of. He was introduced to me by Sir Reginald."

"Enough, sir, I wish to hear nothing more. If you can explain your conduct satisfactorily to-morrow, well and good; but, if not, I beg that you will never again presume to enter the presence of my injured niece. Farewell."

And he went, leaving Percy a prey to feelings of vexation and remorse. Mr. Earl, on his return to Maud, prevailed on her to accompany him home. "I will explain, my darling, when we get home, all that may seem strange to you," he said, "but come, I pray."

Maud did as her uncle asked, for he looked so ill and excited. Besides, she felt no wish to remain, so perplexed was her mind about Percy's strange conduct.

When they arrived at the family mansion in Park Lane, he asked her to join him in a few moments in the library. "For," said he, "I have a long, sad story to tell you, my darling."

In a short time, Maud, having changed her dress, joined her uncle. He was sitting with his face buried in his hands, but, on Maud's entrance, rose, placing a chair for her.

"I don't know whether I do right, my Maud," he said, "to pour into your pure ears a tale of sorrow and sin; but it seems to me the only course open to me to explain what otherwise may seem harsh and unjust in my future conduct. Look at that picture, Maud! it represents a lovely girl, but is not half as lovely as the original.

"When a young man I fell in love with a beautiful actress. Don't start and curl that pretty lip, Maud; she was as pure and spotless as yourself. I prevailed on her to consent to a secret marriage, for I could not bear the world to know I had married an actress, and bitterly did I pay for my sinful pride. I took her to Italy, and for three years I experienced such happiness as seldom falls to the lot of mortal man. My wife I found everything that man could desire, and when she presented me with a daughter, my cup of happiness was overflowing; but it was soon to be dashed from my lips. When my little one was between three and four years old, a young man, almost a boy, travelling with his tutor, came to stay a few weeks in our neighbourhood. We invited him to our house, and in a short time he became quite domesticated with us; but, alas! although he had the face of an angel, he had the heart of a demon, and boy as he was, tried to take my wife from me, but finding that impossible, determined to be revenged on her, and an excellent opportunity occurred.

Business of importance called me to England, and kept me longer than I expected. But I grew very anxious, for I had received no letters from my wife, although I had written several, and hurried back, full of apprehension. When I arrived at our house, the servant told me that my wife and child had left, but there were some letters for me. I rushed up stairs in a frenzy of fear, into my darling's room. There were all her things left, nothing taken. What could it mean? I saw a letter on the table, addressed to me. I tore it open, and read the following:—'Walter, when you read this, I and my child will be sleeping peacefully under the blue waters of the Mediterranean. I will not reproach you, for you once loved us, and our sad fate will make you suffer sufficiently. Oh, Walter! would to God I could think it a dream, but your own words are, alas, too fearfully distinct. I cannot live a life of disgrace. I could not endure the reproaches of my child when she grew up and learnt the awful truth; and yet God knows I am guiltless. Why had you no pity on my youth and love? I feel my brain giving way. God have mercy on my soul. I cannot curse you. Farewell, Walter. Your broken-hearted Eva.'

" I read the letter through, and then for the first time recognized another, in apparently my own handwriting. It was a cruel, heartless, cold-blooded note, stating that our marriage was a false one; that I had gone to England, and should never see her more, and whatever money she required, would be sent through my solicitor, winding up with the advice for her to return to her former life, and forget the writer. I read this, and remembered nothing more, and for weeks my life was despaired of, but a strong constitution triumphed, and I rose from a sick bed, no longer the Walter Earl of former days. All happiness seemed crushed out of me. I had but one desire, and that was to find the inventor of the forged letter, and be revenged on him for my lost happiness. I found him at last in the boy I had treated with hospitality. He gloried in the deed, and from his lips I heard the reason. I called him out; he wounded me

7

and escaped, and I retired to the place made sacred by my former happiness. Besides, as I walked by the Mediterranean, I almost fanced my darlings hovered near me. Years passed in this way, until a feverish longing to be loved by some one belonging to me induced me to come to England and see the child of my dead sister. I found her everything I could wish, and you have bestowed on a broken-hearted man more happiness, my darling, than you can ever have any idea of. But the reason I tell you this sad story to-night is this, the man who was last night with Percy Lysle, his chosen companion, is the ruthless destroyer of my happiness! Am I right then in saying that if Percy cannot explain his conduct fully, he must never enter your presence more? I know I am asking you to offer up a fearful sacrifice; but my Maud, loved daughter of a still more dearly loved sister, I would rather see you dead than married to a companion of Algernon Lance."

For some minutes after Mr. Earl had finished speaking, Maud felt like a person in a dream. The strange, sad story she had heard, and the request to give up Percy could not, she felt, be true; but soon some of the Clayton pride came to her assistance, and looking in Mr. Earl's face she said:—"If Mr. Lysle cannot give a satisfactory account of his conduct, I will see him no more."

The hard, cold tone in which these words were uttered, so unlike Maud's usually sweet voice, stung her uncle as though an adder had bitten him, and she saw the sad, agonized expression on his face, her pride gave way, and, throwing herself into his arms, she sobbed as though her heart would break. Mr. Earl did not check her tears, knowing they would relieve her over-charged heart, and at last she became more composed, and bidding her uncle good night, retired to her room to pass the night in tears.

As for Percy, after Mr. Earl had left him, he felt crushed to the earth with shame, for now he saw plainly how despicable his conduct had been; but his infatuation for the woman to whom he had never even spoken was

so strong that he almost rejoiced at the prospect of
being free. "Maud is far too good for me," he said to
himself; "I should never have made her happy," but do
what he would, he could not overcome the unpleasant
feeling that he had behaved like a scoundrel, besides for-
feiting the respect of all good and honourable men, and
that from henceforth his friends and companions must
be among the Lances and Greens, and others of that
vampire set. He returned to his box in anything but
an amiable frame of mind, and not all the wit of his
associate could bring a smile to his face. He was
aroused, however, by an exclamation from Lance.

"What is the matter?" said Percy.

"Nothing; only a resemblance to some one I knew
years ago."

Percy was surprised to see Lance look disconcerted,
and following the direction of his eyes saw them rest on
a pale, beautiful girl in the box opposite.

"Who can she be?" thought Percy, but no recollection of her features crossed his memory, or perhaps he
would have remembered that her face caused strange
emotion to Mr. Earl two years before, for it was no
other than Ella who occupied the box, with Mrs. Wilton.
The sight of her seemed to exercise strange power over
Algernon Lance, for he who had been witty and sarcastic,
suddenly became silent and preoccupied, and on Ella
rising to leave hastily, he left Percy, saying he should
be back in a few moments. All this struck Percy as
very strange, and he determined to find out the meaning
of his guardian's words, so on Lance's return, he asked
him in a careless, off-hand way if he had ever met a man
named Walter Earl? Algernon Lance started as though
a thunder-bolt had fallen at his feet, but his wonted self-
possession soon returned, and he replied, "Yes, he had
once met a man of that name, but many years ago."

"You must have been very young then?"

"Yes; I was not so old as you are."

"But you are not a very old man," said Percy, returning to the charge, "and many years ago, as you call
it, must have seen in you a child."

7—2

"I am older than you think; but suppose we drop the subject. The reminiscences it conjures up are none of the most agreeable."

Lance spoke in such a hard, cold voice, quite unlike his accustomed winning tones, that Percy said no more, but for all that, made up his mind to unravel the mystery. Lance pleading fatigue, bade Percy good night at the close of the performance, although they had arranged to sup together, but Percy was not sorry to be quit of his society, for a feeling of suspicion had crept into his mind which Mr. Earl's words and Lance's manner had increased.

CHAPTER XI.

THE HEART STRUGGLE.

ALL that night Percy lay awake, thinking over what had passed, and making resolutions as to the future. At one moment he felt half glad to have regained his freedom; then he was overcome with a sense of shame at his conduct, and ultimately his better angel triumphed.

"Shall I," he asked of himself, "throw myself at Maud's feet, confessing my falsehood, beg her to forgive and release me, or manfully fulfil my engagement, and strive by making her happy to efface my dishonour? Why do I ask? My duty plainly points out the road for me to follow, and henceforth I will live for another's happiness. I will overcome this infatuation that enthrals me. Maud shall never know that my heart was another's. I will consecrate my life to her."

From the moment Percy had resolved to follow this course, he felt more peaceful than he had done for weeks. The morning saw him at Park Lane; Mr. Earl received him, and Percy having nerved himself for the task, plunged boldly into it, confessing all that the reader already knows, except his infatuation for Cora. Mr. Earl heard him to the end, and then gave him an account of all he knew of Algernon Lance's life, touching but lightly on the story he had told Maud the previous night.

"At eighteen he was a villain," he said, "and as he grew in years, from all accounts, he did not mend. An only son with a large fortune, he squandered it all away, even before he came of age, and then he preyed on his fellow-men. At one place in Germany, he was leagued with a band of ruffians who were supposed even not to have stopped short of the murder of those who had won large sums of money. It could not legally be found out, but so fearful were people of him, and so vigilantly was he watched, that he was obliged to leave. He was then lost sight of for several years, and then turned up in Paris, where he again by unfair means won a large sum of money from a young man almost a boy, whose all it was, and who was driven to committing suicide. After that he was compelled to leave France, and now I again see him in your society. I am willing to believe that you were totally unaware of his character; but had you asked any one, they could have told you enough of Algernon Lance's villainy to have put you on your guard. But let this be a lesson, and remember that should you ever again fall under his fascinations, you will have sacrificed my friendship, for never could I clasp the hand that had grasped in friendliness that of my deadly enemy. He robbed me of wife and child, and made life a burden to me; and even if I could forgive, the memory of their sufferings would prevent me. See, that is the portrait of the woman he drove to death."

Percy took the miniature, and almost let it fall when he recognized the likeness to the lady in the box, who had attracted Lance's attention.

"Are you sure she died?" he demanded.

"Why do you ask?" said Mr. Earl; "for God's sake speak!"

"Because I could swear that the original of this picture was in the theatre last night. And what is more, Lance's exclamation first called my attention to her. He said she reminded him of an old friend of his, known years before."

" Great God! can it be possible that Eva lives, and that I have mourned for her all these years ? Fool that I have been to calmly take for granted that she perished ; and yet, alas, there is no hope, I fear. No, it can only be a passing likeness, and my darlings are under the blue waves. But should they live! I dare not think of it ; it is too much happiness, and the disappointment would kill me ; but, Percy, make all inquiries ; find out where she lives, this likeness of my lost Eva."

" I will," said Percy, " but first let me see Maud, and ask her forgiveness ?"

" Certainly."

The servant entered with the message that Miss Clayton awaited Mr. Lysle in the drawing-room. On entering the room, Percy was startled at the change in Maud, whom he had not seen for more than two months ; the eyes were as bright as usual, but there were dark rings round them ; the cheeks were too flushed for health, and her face looked thin.

" I did not know that you had been ill, Maud," said Percy, his heart smiting him as he spoke, for he saw in this but another evidence of the effects of his conduct.

" It is nothing," replied Maud, " but a bad cold, I have had these two months. I think I told you of it in a letter I wrote you some time since."

She spoke in a constrained voice, but Percy could see that she was suffering.

" Maud," he said, " I have a most humiliating confession to make ; and if, after hearing it, you can still trust me with your happiness, I will strive to be worthy of you."

He then told about his broken word to her and Mr. Earl, his acquaintance with Lance, and the gambling transactions. While he spoke he dared not look at Maud, knowing how he had wronged her ; but when he had finished, the loving girl threw herself into his arms, saying,—" I felt sure, Percy, dear, that it was not your fault, and that all could be explained. It would have broken my heart if it had not been so; do you know, Percy, that I could not stay at the Towers without letters from you, and I should not care to live without your love."

As Percy looked into that pleading, upturned face, gazing so trustfully into his own, all his better nature triumphed, and he registered a vow that, no matter what he might suffer, she should never know she had not his undivided heart.

" This is the woman," thought Percy, " I calmly made up my mind to sacrifice for a selfish infatuation; if I give her my life I can scarcely repay her for her angelic trust and devotion. Maud, darling," at last, said Percy, " can you trust me so far as to be my wife immediately, if Mr. Earl will consent? I feel, dear, that, with you to guide me I could not go wrong. I have a weak, wavering nature ; but with you for my guardian angel, to support me with your love and trust, I should be strong."

Maud hid her face in his breast and gave consent. Percy felt happier than he ever thought to be, since henceforth he should have some one to live for, and he had put an insurmountable barrier between himself and Cora. To think of her now would be a crime to one who loved him with her whole heart, and whose life hung on his truth.

Full of these thoughts, Percy left Maud, to ask Mr. Earl's consent. He found him pacing the library with impatient steps, but the old man stopped when Percy entered. At first, Mr. Earl looked grave, but at last acceded to Percy's pleading, stipulating for a delay of two months longer before the marriage should take place.

" Leave her with me that time, Percy, and prove that you are worthy of possessing the greatest treasure that ever fell to man's lot, a woman's loving heart."

Percy saw that Mr. Earl was in earnest, so had to consent with a good grace, and that day two months was fixed for the wedding.

When it was all settled, Mr. Earl turned to his nephew, and reminded him of his promise to find out the lady of the theatre.

"Remember, Percy," he said, "you are taking my niece, who is all I have to love, from me; therefore you are bound to help me to find news of my lost ones : but I am indulging in hopes, alas, I fear never to be realized!"

"Well, sir," was Percy's reply, "we can but make enquiries: so keep up your heart, and farewell until evening, when I hope to bring you some news."

When Percy left Park Lane, he hardly knew how to set about performing the task he had undertaken, when at last the thought struck him that to enquire at the box-office the name of the people who took that box would be the wisest plan.

Accordingly, he called a cab, and was soon at the theatre. In answer to his enquiries, the box-keeper said that Mrs. Wilton (Cora's mother) occupied it in company with a young lady, a friend; but who she was he did not know.

"Can you give me Mrs. Wilton's address," asked Percy.

"Yes, sir; here it is: 3, Adelina Terrace, Hyde Park."

Percy gave the man a sovereign, and was soon rattling along in a Hansom in that direction. He had no difficulty in finding the house, and a few minutes found him at the door of Cora's abode.

His heart beat as he thought of seeing Cora and hearing her speak; but the remembrance of a sweet loving face, that had rested on his heart but one short hour before, made him strong, and when the door was opened he had conquered his emotion. Mrs. Wilton was at home, the servant said, in answer to his enquiry; would he walk into the drawing-room, and she would take his card to her? Percy did so. The maid departed on her errand, and he was left alone. This, then, was the house of the brilliant actress, — a very commonplace one. There stood her piano, and if one might judge by the pieces of music, she was not a finished musician. Three or four portraits represented her in her different characters, and one in private costume. Tennyson and Byron adorned the little centre table, and a pretty good bust of Shakspeare stood on the mantel-shelf. A few flowers, artistically arranged, completed the ornaments of the room, except a canary, in a bright cage, who began singing when Percy entered, as though to welcome him. That room, with its few attractions, never faded from Percy's memory, and in after years he could recall to mind the exact position of each article it contained. He was not detained long, when a lady entered, whom he had not the slightest difficulty in recognising, from her likeness to her daughter, as Mrs. Wilton. He made known the cause of his visit, saying that a friend of his being struck with the likeness of a lady, who was in the box with Mrs. Wilton last evening, to a dear friend of his, he had taken the liberty of calling on her to enquire the name of the lady. Mrs. Wilton looked grave, and Percy saw that the only way to gain the information he required would be to interest Mrs. Wilton's sympathies, which he accordingly did, by telling her part of the story, suppressing all names, and he was rewarded by the grave look being replaced by one of interest.

"Well," said she, when Percy had finished his recital, now you have explained, why you wished to gain the information, I will tell you all I know ; but stay, my daughter, Cora, whose friend she is, can tell you better, so I will send for her, if you please."

Cora soon after made her appearance in answer to her mother's summons, and when she saw Percy she started and blushed, for she remembered his brown eyes.

"This gentleman, dear, wishes to know all we can tell him about Ella, because some one he knows is so much struck by her likeness to a dear friend of his who disappeared some years since." So said the mother.

Cora then gave Percy the history of Ella, as far as she knew. Poor Percy! It was very trying to him to listen to those silver tones ; and if he thought her lovely on the stage, she looked in his eyes ten times more so now. By a firm control over himself he prevented the slightest sign of admiration, so he thought, to escape, but women are very penetrating, and before Cora had been in

the room ten minutes she knew that Percy loved her in
spite of his studied indifference. Mrs. Wilton, who was
very interested, gave Ella's address, and begged him to
come again and tell her if he found that Ella was any
relation to the person he supposed. Having no further
excuse for prolonging his visit, Percy bade adieu to
Adelina Terrace ; but his heart was heavy. Having seen
Cora and having spoken to her, instead of dispelling his
infatuation, had riveted his chains more tightly,—but the
die was cast. He was the promised husband of another,
and he must tear her image from his heart ; but in spite
of all his endeavours a vision of violet eyes and golden
curls would rise up before him.

Camden Town, with its labyrinth of shabby little
streets, the refuge of genteel poverty, is even at the best
of times dismal and depressing ; but on a dark, rainy
November day, it is fearfully dispiriting. It was so on
this the first time Percy had ever visited it.

"Is it possible that people can live in such a neighbourhood!" he thought to himself. "For my part, I
should either go melancholy mad or commit suicide in a
week. Let me see, the address is Prospect Place."

By this time the cab had stopped at the beginning of
a small row of houses.

"This is the place, sir ; but what number ?" asked the
cabman.

Percy looked at the houses, and thought there must be
some mistake, they seemed so forlorn and wretched ; but
there was the name surely enough, so it must be right.

"No. 12, I think it is ; but it is a shop of some kind,"
he said.

The cabman resumed his seat.

"What ever could bring such a swell to Prospect Place,
Camden Town," he thought. "There's No. 12, sir."

"All right," said Percy, "wait for me ;" and he hurried into the shop—if a little front parlour could be dig-
nified with such a title.

Old Mrs. Brown, who was sitting working, was startled
by the unusual appearance of a gentleman. "And such
a gentleman!" as she said, in her shop, and stood curt-

seying, anxious to know what she could sell him out of her penny publications. But she was doomed to disappointment, when he enquired if she had a lady named Graham living in her house.

"Yes, sir, but she's dreadful bad; not able to get out of doors at all this three weeks, poor soul! Be you any relation, sir?"

"No," said Percy.

"Beg your pardon, no offence; but Mrs. Graham is quite the lady, and I thought maybe she'd quarrelled with her friends, and come here to live alone with her two children. At least that's what Mrs. Sparks, who lives over the way, said; but I says to her, I says, 'she's a real lady, whatever it is, but that quiet and reserved like that one couldn't ask her.'"

Percy saw the good woman was a gossip, and at any other time would have been amused at her loquacity; but he now felt too much preoccupied to attend to her, and cut short a long story she was beginning by desiring her to enquire if Mrs. Graham would see a gentleman on important business? In a few moments Mrs. Brown returned with permission, and Percy mounted the rickety stairs to Mrs. Graham's rooms. It was an affecting scene that Percy looked upon. A woman was sitting in an armchair by the window, propped up with pillows. A little girl, with dark, mournful eyes, was sitting at her feet, holding one of her poor wasted hands; while a tall girl, just emerged from girlhood, had evidently been reading to the invalid.

"Pardon my intrusion," said Percy, "but I come on business of importance."

Ella, for it was she who had been reading, rose, and placing a chair for Percy, resumed her seat near her mother.

"I scarcely know how to begin," said Percy, "but first allow me to ask, did you ever know a Mr. Earl?"

If he had entertained any doubt, it was dispelled by the effect the name had on the invalid.

"Yes, yes," said she, "what of him? Tell me, I pray you, if he lives; tell him I forgive him, and would fain see him again before I leave this world."

"He does live," said Percy ; "but can you bear a great surprise—a great joy ?"

"Alas! what joy can come to me in this world, save to see him once again, and hear he has repented the wrong he did me years ago."

"He has no cause to repent ; you were his lawful wife, who believed the false tongue of a villain, and accepted a clumsy forgery, against all the love and devotion of years."

"Great God! what is this I hear! Have I wronged him all these years ? But, impossible! Proofs, young man ; give me pooofs ? Do you not see that I am hastening to the grave ? Do not, I implore you, deceive me !"

"I do not, I assure you ; if you are Eva Graham, who twenty years ago married Walter Earl, and lived at San Remo with him."

"I am," interrupted Mrs. Graham, and fainted.

"What have I done," said Percy. "How unfortunate I am. Those I would help I injure."

"Do not distress yourself," said Ella ; "she will revive soon. But tell me, is my father alive, and is this he ?" (placing in Percy's hand the miniature already described).

"Yes, that is he. See, here is the name—Walter Earl. I will go and fetch him, that he may have the happiness of clasping again in his arms those loved ones he thought dead."

Seeing Mrs. Graham was reviving, Percy left, and directed the cabman to Park Lane.

"Drive as fast as you can, and you shall have double fare," he said.

"All right, sir ; I'll drive you faster than any man in London. What's up," thought he, as he got on the box ; "but it's no business of mine, as long as I'm well paid."

The cabman kept his promise, and Percy reached Park Lane in an incredibly short space of time. Mr. Earl was in the library, so the footman said, and Percy bent his steps thither.

"What news ?" asked Mr. Earl, grasping Percy's hand with impatience.

" The best, sir. I have found them ; they live."

For a moment Percy thought Mr. Earl was going to fall ; but he recovered himself.

" Take me to her, Percy, at once, or I shall believe it is all a dream."

" I have a cab waiting, and will take you at once," and in a few moments they were again on the road.

Mr. Earl was silent, his emotions were too strong for words ; but when he saw the dreary houses, he shuddered, and Percy could see the tears running down his cheeks. Prospect Place was soon reached, and the neighbours were startled by the re-appearance of the cab at Mrs. Brown's. Mr. Earl followed Percy upstairs, and stood outside while Percy prepared the invalid for the meeting. As he stood on that narrow, dark landing, with only the door between him and the woman he had thought lost to him for ever, his agitation became extreme ; and although Percy was but a few moments before he reappeared to usher him into the chamber of his wife, the moments seemed hours. Mrs. Graham, or as we must now call her, Mrs. Earl, was sitting propped up by pillows, near the window ; but on the entrance of her husband, she rose, and would have fallen but for his outstretched arms.

Both Ella and Percy left the room, taking Eunice with them ; for the meeting between the two long-severed hearts was too sacred even for a daughter's eye to witness.

At first neither spoke, but Mrs. Earl was the first to recover her composure.

" Forgive me, Walter, for what I have done. Oh, want of faith, what misery has it not caused !"

" Hush ! Eva, wife, do not blame yourself ; rather reproach me for ever leaving you exposed to the fascinations of that monster. But, dear one, we have suffered so much ; let us not cloud the joy of our meeting by regret or reproaches. But tell me how you escaped death ?"

" It is a long and miserable story, Walter ; but I will summon strength and courage to tell it you. Soon after you left me, young Lance, boy as he was, began perse-cuting me with his vile addresses, and at last when I bade him leave the house, laughed at me, telling me he

had your permission to remain, and I had no power.
What could I do, a woman alone, but shut myself in my own
rooms and await your return? Days passed into weeks,
and though I wrote letter after letter to you, I received
no answer. At last, when almost in despair, one came.
I broke the seal, and read that which turned my brain to
fire : 'I was not your wife!' At first my mind refused
to believe it, but the words left no room for doubt, and
then all became dark,—I had fainted. When I recovered
it was evening, and little Ella, who was by my side, had
evidently cried herself to sleep, as the tears were still on
her cheeks. For a few moments I could not collect my
scattered thoughts ; but, at the sight of the letter, the
dreadful truth came back with fearful intensity. I made
up my mind not to live, and wrote you a letter enclosing
the one from you, which had turned the sunshine of my
life into tears and madness. Taking up my child, who
was still sleeping, I wrapped her in a shawl and left the
house. It was dark, and we were unobserved. I rushed
to the beach, my only thought being to put an end to
my wretched existence, and plunged into the sea. A
confused murmur in my ears, and I lost all consciousness ;
but I was not to end my sinful life in that way, for some
fishermen happened to be passing, and seeing my light
dress, rescued me and my child, and on returning to life,
as it were, I found myself in a small fishing smack. My
first feelings were those of gratitude to the all-merciful
providence who had saved me from being a murderess ;
for Ella was by my side, and I determined to live and
work for her. One of the men who had rescued us came
in the little cabin, and in him I found a man whom I had
helped at San Remo. He knew me, and offered to put
me on shore directly, but I begged him to land me a little
farther along, and as they were going to Nice, they took
me along with them. I had some articles of jewellery
about me, and by the sale of those in Nice I hoped to
pay our passage to England and give something to our
preservers. At Nice I went to a very modest locanda,
and begged the landlord to negociate the sale of my
trinkets, which consisted of my watch and chain, a very

valuable ring you gave me, and your portrait, which was in my brooch; but that I could not part with, so kept it. The landlord was honest, and brought me their value, sixty pounds. My preservers refused to take any of my money, and I left in a sailing vessel for England."

Here a fit of coughing prevented Mrs. Earl from speaking for several moments, but presently she resumed her narrative:

"We arrived in England, and I resumed my profession and name, and obtained an engagement; but I was no longer the Eva Graham of former days, I had lost all joyousness and hope; life seemed to me a hard, stern reality. I was always cold and repelling, almost defiant. I thought that people guessed my secret and were pitying me when they were kind; the very thought drove me mad. At last I met a man named Lawrence, a tragedian. He was deferential in his manner, and at last won my consent to become his wife. I did not love him, but I believed him to be good and honourable. Thinking that my life would be short, I married him that I might have a protector for my beloved child. But before I had been his wife a week I found out the dreadful mistake I had made. He was coarse and brutal. Ella was even sent on the stage to help to support his extravagance, and I was his slave, beaten when in his drunken humours I thwarted him. But my misery was not of long duration, for after the birth of Eunice I lost my voice, and, finding me no longer able to earn money, my tyrant left us to starve. I managed to support myself and children by becoming dresser at the theatre, and Ella after a time entered the ballet, and took my place as provider of our daily bread, for my health broke down entirely then, and ever since she has supported us."

For some time after this story was ended not a word was spoken, but Mrs. Earl broke the silence.

"Walter, forgive me," said she, and before her husband could prevent her, she had fallen on her knees before him.

"My darling, do not stay there; come to my heart,

my poor injured Eva, and let the past be forgotten ; live for my sake and that of the children."

" No, my husband, that is impossible, the fiat has gone forth that I must die, but the happiness I now experience is worth a life-time of misery. Besides, Walter, it is better I should die for your sake ; but make me quite happy by promising to take care of Eunice as well as Ella. I do not expect you to love her, but protect her, and let her sometimes see her sister, for, poor little thing, she has a loving, affectionate nature, and although she is the child of a cruel taskmaster, she is mine, and I love her dearly."

The tears were rolling fast down the poor mother's cheeks as she pleaded for her child, and Mr. Earl thought, as he looked in that beloved face, that he would gladly grant any request to bring peace to that broken heart.

" I will take her, Eva, and for your sake she shall be as dear to me as my own daughter. Henceforth I have two children to love and protect."

" Thanks, thanks ; you have taken a load of sorrow from my heart, call in the children and let them rejoice in their happiness."

Ella, who was waiting outside for a summons, gladly entered with Eunice.

" And Percy," said Mr. Earl, " this is my wife, these are my two daughters."

Percy wondered how that could be, but he said nothing. Mr. Earl was rewarded for his goodness by the look of love and gratitude in the wan features of his wife, and little Eunice crept up to him and kissed his hand. The action was a simple one, but it did more than all the most demonstrative affection could have effected, it opened the flood-gates of Mr. Walter Earl's kindly nature, and he clasped the little thing to his heart, as he registered a solemn vow to be indeed a parent to her.

" And you, Ella, come to me, my darling," said Mr. Earl, as he put Eunice down, and held out his arms for his daughter.

Ella complied, and in that embrace Ella's reserve

melted away, and she returned her father's caress with fervour.

"Percy," at last said Mr. Earl, "what am I to do, I cannot leave my recovered treasures here, but where shall we go? I cannot take them to Park Lane without first apprizing my niece, Maud, and I know of no other place."

"I shall be most happy if Mrs. Earl and her daughters will occupy my rooms for the present," was the answer.

"I thank you very much. I will accept your offer for them."

"Very well then, I will go and see that everything is got ready for their reception."

"Stay, dear husband," said the invalid, "I have not strength to move from here. The exertion would curtail the few short days I have to live. Wait until I am no more, and then remove my children, but in the meantime give me as much of your beloved society as you can."

"Eva, you must live for my sake, it is too hard to find you again only to lose you. I cannot bear it."

"Stay, darling Walter, listen to me, it is better thus, we shall only be parted for a while, and meet again in a brighter, better world than this; believe me, it is for the best, and you will have the consolation of knowing that you made the last days of my life truly happy, and lifted the weight of fear and doubt from my heart. I am tired now, and will rest a little, but, Walter, do not leave me for long."

"I will never leave you again, darling," said Mr. Earl, as he kissed the pale forehead of his wife, "but I must go and find a doctor, and, Eva, you must recover; my love shall snatch you even from the gates of death."

Mrs. Earl said nothing, for she could not endure to dispel all his hopes, but when he was gone she prayed long and fervently that the Giver of all Good would grant him strength to bear the parting so soon to come.

8

CHAPTER XII.

THE OLD HOUSE BY THE RIVER.

PERCY LYSLE'S visit to Adelina Terrace had the result of making Cora very thoughtful, and several times she caught herself wondering if she should see the owner of the brown eyes again. Cora would scarcely have been a woman had she not felt flattered at the admiration he evidently felt for her, in spite of his attempt to conceal it; but although gratified vanity has a great effect on the mind, it could hardly have brought such rosy blushes to Cora's cheeks at the mere mention of his name.

The day passed, evening came, and Percy was not at the theatre, and Cora felt a kind of disappointment at not seeing him. But when several days elapsed, and still he came not, she grew impatient, and fretful without cause. Her mother wondered, for Cora generally had a very sweet temper. What could be the cause of this change? A week had gone by in this unsatisfactory state of things, when one night a card was brought to Cora in the green room. It bore the name of "Sir Reginald Clayton." Her cheeks flushed as she read the name. How dare he persist in persecuting her thus? She was going to send and say that she could not see the gentleman in question, when a few words pencilled on the back attracted her attention. "Sir Reginald has a message of importance from a friend of Miss Wilton's."

"A friend of mine," said Cora. "Well, perhaps, I had better see what it is. Where is the gentleman?" she asked, addressing the box-keeper, who brought the card.

"In the hall, miss."

"Very well, I will see him," and Cora followed the man to the stage entrance.

Sir Reginald was standing with his back towards the door that led from the stage.

"You have a message for me, I believe, Sir Reginald. From whom, and what is its nature?"

Sir Reginald started as the voice of the woman he had so madly loved fell on his ear, but he stifled his emotions in an instant, and greated Cora with a bland smile.

"Yes, Miss Wilton, I have a message from my cousin, Percy Lysle."

It was now Cora's turn to start and change colour, and it was not lost on Sir Reginald; a fiendish look passed over his face, but by the time Cora had regained her self-possession, it had quite faded away, and was replaced by a calm quiet smile.

"I had no idea that Mr. Lysle was a relation of yours, but he is scarcely a friend of mine, Sir Reginald Clayton. I have been anxious to hear from him some news of a dear friend of mine, and no doubt the message you bring concerns her."

"Of that I do not know, Miss Wilton; but he bade me say that he had succeeded, and would send you particulars."

"Thank him, and say I am very glad. And now, good evening, as I have to go on the stage in a few moments. Thank you also for bringing me such satisfactory news."

With these words Cora left Sir Reginald a prey to not very enviable feelings. Lighting a cigar, and bidding the hall-keeper good evening, he strolled forth into the night air.

"She loves that boy," he said, "and I who would have sacrificed my life for her, am despised; but I will be revenged. That weak, puling boy, how I hate him! We Claytons are good haters, and he is not the first who will rue crossing my path. And that meddling fool, Walter Earl, I owe him a grudge for his warning to his precious ward, Percy. But what, I wonder, can make Lance so bitter with him. It is no affair of mine; if Algernon but helps me with Cora. I must see him and arrange to-night."

Sir Reginald turned into the Albany. Algernon Lance was at home, and evidently expecting his visitor.

"Did you see her?" he asked, after Sir Reginald entered and carefully closed the door.

" Yes, and told her that particulars would be sent in a few days. She loves that fellow, Lance ; I saw it in her face when I mentioned his name. I could have killed her where she stood !"

The strong man clenched his teeth with agony, as he spoke. Algernon Lance looked on with calm indifference and surprise. He could not understand Sir Reginald's passionate, impulsive nature, so different to his own calculating, cold-blooded one. Besides, his estimate of women was a very low one.

" Love him, Clayton ?" he said, with a sneer ; " she will soon get over that. When she sees there is no chance she will accept her fate. I never met but one woman who could not be won with gold or flattery, and she was unlike her sex in general."

A heavy cloud sat on Captain Lance's brow as he spoke ; but it did not rest there long, and his features regained their wonted look of well-bred indifference.

" Enough of sentimentality," said Sir Reginald at last, going to a sideboard and pouring out a glass of brandy as he spoke. " To business ; this house you spoke of, is it secure ?"

" As the grave," and Captain Lance gave a little laugh. " But to-morrow you shall see it. Your fair Cora may cry for help for a month, and no one will hear her except the ghosts, of which there are a score."

" But how came you to know of it ?"

" Listen, old boy, and I will tell you. Some years ago I got into trouble about a duel, and had to fly ; but the relations of the man raised a hue and cry all over England. The seaports were watched, and I was in a fix, when my servant (you have seen him) came to my rescue, and told me about this house. How he heard of it I never enquired, but gladly followed his advice, and hid there until the affair blew over. Not that I enjoyed my sojourn there, I can tell you ; and if your cruel *inamorata* only experiences my feelings, it will soon bring her to her senses. I think I should have given myself up rather than remain another week in that place."

" Did you see any ghosts there ?" asked Sir Reginald,

and a little sneer was perceptible in the tone of his voice, for he was incredulous, and being bold as a lion himself, had no sympathy with fear in a man, no matter from what source it might spring.

"Yes, I did," was the answer. "Ah! you may laugh, Clayton; but I did see strange things," and Algernon Lance grew positively ghastly at the remembrance.

"Let us go to-night, Lance, and I will defy all the ghosts in Christendom!"

"No."

"But I say 'yes;' it will help to kill time. Besides, it will create less suspicion visiting it at night; so come along, old fellow."

Algernon Lance tried all in his power to dissuade his friend, but in vain. The brandy he had taken prevented his listening to any arguments, however specious; so seeing there was no help for it, he rang the bell for Joe White, and in a very short time they were rolling along in a cab with Joe on the box. It was late—past ten; most of the shops were shut, and all was dark, save here and there where a bright glare of light proclaimed the gin palace; anon these signs of life grew less frequent, and Sir Reginald perceived that they were leaving the great city behind them.

"How much further is this ghostly mansion?" demanded he of Lance.

"Not very far; but we shall have to walk presently. We cannot drive all the way, because it is down a lane."

After these observations, each relapsed into silence. Another half-hour passed, and the cab stopped.

"We get out here," said Captain Lance, as Joe got down and opened the door. "You had better tell the cabman to wait for us, Joe; and now follow me."

He turned off the road into a narrow lane. There was a bright moon that night, but even her silver rays could not enliven the scene Sir Reginald looked upon: flat marshy fields, unrelieved by trees, with pools of stagnant water glistening in the moonlight. After walking some minutes, they arrived within sight of the river, and a tall, desolate house broke on Sir Reginald's view.

"We have arrived at our destination," said Captain Lance, as he halted before some high iron gates. "What think you of this place? Will it do?"

"It's dull enough for anything," replied his friend, "but let's see the interior, before I can judge."

"You shall soon be gratified. Here, Joe, open these gates."

Joe, thus admonished, produced a key from his pocket, and the gates rolled back on their hinges with a creaking, ghastly sound. For a moment something like pity for the fate he was preparing for Cora took possession of Sir Reginald's heart; but the remembrance of her scorn banished it almost immediately, and he determined to carry out his wicked designs at all hazards. The gates closed, and Sir Reginald found himself in a paved court, dank and dreary, like a long disused graveyard. A flight of steps led up to the entrance, which had once been handsome, but now everything wore the same aspect of ruin and desolation.

"If the interior only corresponds with the exterior, what a charming place to rusticate in this would be!" said Sir Reginald with a laugh, which sounded hollow and forced, even to himself.

"Well, you shall soon have an opportunity of judging of its advantages," replied Captain Lance, as he unlocked the door and ushered Sir Reginald into the hall. "Close the door; and Joe, be quick with the light. Ah! that's right. Now, Clayton, you follow me; Joe, you stay here and wait for us."

Captain Lance conducted Sir Reginald up a wide flight of stairs, hung with the cobwebs of many years. After going nearly to the top he stopped, and unlocking a door, motioned to Sir Reginald to enter.

"There, Clayton, what think you of this as a cage for your pretty bird?" he asked. "She may beat her wings against the bars, but she will not get free when once in, I'll answer for it."

The room was large and, like the rest of the house, was old-fashioned. and when in its best days must have been gloomy enough. Now it was melancholy beyond description. A whole colony of rats scampered away as they entered.

"By Jove, Lance, it's scarcely the place; it's too bad. The girl might go mad here all alone."

"At any rate you can keep her company, and with your courage and love to protect her, what will she have to fear? Take my word for it, even hating you like death, after a few hours' solitary meditation in this room she will hail even your presence with joy," and Lance laughed his little silver laugh.

Sir Reginald with all his wickedness shuddered at the thought of consigning Cora to such a fate, even though her scorn of him had turned all his love to blackest hate, but the devil in the person of Algernon Lance, was there to urge him on.

"Of course," he said, "this room will be made habitable, Joe will see to that; but don't you think we had better be going?"

Was it fancy, or did Algernon Lance change colour as a long wail broke on their ears?

"Why, man," said Sir Reginald, "how scared you look; it's only the wind."

'Very likely, but let's be going, the place is so cold and damp," and Lance hurried out of the room, followed by Sir Reginald.

The cab was waiting, and in a short time the dreary neighbourhood of Battersea was left behind. Few words were spoken, for both Captain Lance and Sir Reginald were engrossed with their own thoughts, but by the time they arrived at the Albany they had recovered their spirits.

"I wonder what those swells were up to?" said the cabman, when he drove away, pocketing his fare, "that lane led no where except to the river and Helsdon House. They cannot have gone there, and yet who knows? It's not always the whitest hands that's most free from stains, and perhaps they have some black work to do, and think that the fittest place to do it in. At any rate I'll keep an eye on them, and who knows, I may find out something that may be worth a mine o' money to me, and help me in my search after that villain who tried to swear my life away; something in the servant's voice who sat by my side on the box reminded me of him, but it can't be. No, no, I must look further afield."

Suppose he had known what passed at the Albany?

"Why, Joe, how ill you look," said Lance, as the light in the hall shone on his servant's face, and disclosed his features convulsed with abject terror. "Did you see any ghosts in the old house?"

"No, sir," he stammered, "but I don't feel well, and would like to go to bed, if you can spare me."

"All right, go. We will manage without you."

Sir Reginald and his companion went into the diningroom, where a night-fire was burning, and Joe White crept up the stairs to his room. The face which met his in the looking-glass startled him with its ghastly expression of horror, and he rushed from it and sank down on his bed in an agony of terror.

"He has come back," he gasped out, "after all these years. He will kill me; he swore he would, and will keep his word. Perhaps he did not know me, and yet I saw him start when I spoke. Ah! there is no mistake: he will hunt me down."

"I will let you know," said Lance, as he bade Sir Reginald good night, "when the thing is arranged. Leave it all to me until Thursday. Good bye."

Some days had elapsed since Sir Reginald's interview with Cora, and she was surprised one day to receive a letter from Percy Lysle, which ran as follows:

"You must pardon my taking the liberty of writing to you; but your friend, Ella, has been and is in such sad trouble by the death of her mother, that her father is in despair about her, and as a last resource I have written to beg you will come and see her, and try if the presence of an old friend will not rouse her from the lethargic state into which she has now fallen. My servant brings this note, and will wait for an answer, or if you will come my carriage is at your service and will bring you here and return again with you. Once more asking your pardon, believe me, yours truly, Percy Lysle."

Cora took the letter to her mother, and Mrs. Wilton was anxious her daughter should go and see her old friend.

"Where is the place—Ramsdon House, Clapham. Well, I have no doubt it is all right; but I wish your father was at home to go with you. Shall I accompany you?"

"No, thank you, dear mother; there is nothing to fear, and it is clearly my duty to go to poor Ella. I shall be back by four."

With this Cora rang the bell, and directed the girl to tell the man who brought the letter to wait for her, as her mistress would go with him. In a few moments Cora was ready, and if any misgivings had crossed her mind, the respectable appearance of the old man-servant would have dispelled them at once, and Cora jumped into the brougham, and was soon rolling away at a good pace. She had no knowledge of the district through which she was passing, but the dismal, dreary waste-lands, dotted with boards advertising it for eligible building purposes, and the cheerless tracks, never calcu-lated to inspire one with feelings of pleasure, now seen under the dispiriting influence of a foggy December afternoon, had an effect upon Cora, chilling her with a presentiment of evil, which having once taken possession of her she could not easily shake off. Poor Cora, as she whirled along, began wishing that she had waited for her father to have accompanied her; but she was a brave girl, and after a time conquered her fears.

"What have I to be afraid about?" she asked herself.

But the image of Sir Reginald rose before her as he had looked that day when he had sworn vengeance against her, and her nervousness so overcame her that she was about to beg the coachman to return, when he got down and opened the carriage-door. No house was in sight, and Cora was wondering what was the matter, when the man asked her to get out and walk.

"For Miss Ella is so ill, Miss, that the noise of wheels is forbidden by the doctors, and Master Percy said he knew the young lady would not mind walking a few hundred yards on that account."

"Certainly not," said Cora; for the man's respectful manner, and his calling Percy "master," quite reassured her. "He is no doubt an old attached servant of the family," she thought; and laughing at her fears, sprang out of the carriage and followed the old man.

"What a very dull place to live in," she remarked.

"Yes, Miss, it is; but you see Mr. Earl had this house, and when he found his wife, he moved her here at once, because you see it's near town, and as it was only for a short time it did not matter, for the poor lady was too ill to see out of doors and the inside is very comfortable."

By this time, Cora and her conductor had arrived at the iron gates of the haunted house by the river.

"Is this Ramsdon House?" said Cora, with a shudder, "and does poor Ella live here? What a ghostly place, to be sure!"

The tall gates swung back, and Cora entered the court in front of the house; the flag-stones had once been white, but were now green and discoloured from the damp weeds and grass, the growth of years, which covered them. It was a place to shun, and Cora felt her courage flying fast, and but for very shame would have retreated even then. The next moment, and it was too late, for the door was opened by an old woman, and she was ushered into the hall, but little altered since Sir Reginald visited it save that some of the cobwebs had been removed, in the feeble attempt at making it a little tidy. As the door closed, the utter loneliness of her position struck her for the first time.

"Where is Miss Graham?" she asked.

"This way, please;" and the woman pointed to the staircase, which she mounted, Cora following with a beating heart, until they reached an open door on the first landing.

"If you will wait there," she said, "I will fetch Miss Graham."

Cora walked into the room. A candle was alight on the table, and a fire burnt brightly in the grate, shedding its cheery warmth around the room. Cora was cold and tired, and the cheerful rays encouraged her sinking heart, she approached the fire, and sitting down, awaited the appearance of Ella. But time passed and no Ella came. Cora began to feel uneasy, she took out her watch and found that one hour had elapsed since her arrival. She looked about the room for a bell, but there was not one, so she went to the door to call; but what was her agony when she found it fastened on the outside!

CHAPTER XIII.

A FRIEND IN NEED.

ON making this terrible discovery all Cora's former fears returned with renewed force, and she sank into a chair, utterly overcome. After a time, however, she summoned her strength of mind, and taking the candle in her hand, prepared to examine the room in which she was imprisoned, to see if she could discover any mode of egress, save the door through which she had entered. She tried the windows, but the strong iron bars, and forlorn weed-grown gardens, with the river flowing past, sent a thrill of horror through her nerves, and drawing the curtains, she turned away. In doing this, she noticed, for the first time, a small table, covered with provisions, wine, and a note addressed to herself. She tore it open, and found her worst fears verified. She was in the hands of her enemy, Sir Reginald. All his perfidy and wickedness rose before her, mingling with her own deceit to her mother.

"Oh!" she moaned, "if I had only confessed to my mother, she would have had some clue to my whereabouts, and been able to rescue me from the hands of this wicked man. But now what am I to do! Fool, that I was! I thought my sin punished when I found my idol worthless; forgetting, that deceit like mine, brings with it evil worse than death. I deserve it all! But great God, I beseech you deliver me from this fate."

Sinking on her knees, Cora implored help from the great Power from which it alone could come.

When she arose, she felt better able to collect her energies, and see what had best be done. She took the letter from the floor, where she had flung it, and read it through.

"Cora," it began; "you are in my power. I will be with you this evening, and, on yourself alone, depends your future. Yours, ever, Reginald."

"What does he mean by that?" she cried.

She hated him, and he knew it. More, she loved another. For in that time of peril, when Percy Lysle seemed lost to her for ever, she felt how dear he was to her. As the time drew on when she should have appeared at the theatre, the thought of her mother's anxiety about her added to her sufferings. She paced up and down that ghostly room, her footsteps echoing through the house, striking fear into her very soul.

The hours passed, and Cora felt faint from excitement and want of food; but feared to touch the things on the table, lest they might have been drugged so as to render her powerless. At last. when ten o'clock struck, she thought she heard a knock at the hall-door. In a few moments, rapid steps ascended the stairs. She had no time to think—the door was burst open, and Percy Lysle, pale and agitated, entered the room.

"Thank God, you are found!" he faltered, as he seized her hand. "But, come. No time for explanation. I will tell you all, when we have left this accursed place."

Cora needed no further urging to leave; and grasping the arm of her deliverer, ascended the stairs. They found the door open, and no one to bar their exit.

"Come, Cora, we must run," said Percy, when they got outside the iron gates into the lane; "we are not safe even now until we reach the high road."

A few moments brought them to it without molestation. An empty cab passing at the time, Percy hailed it, directing the man where to drive, and handing Cora in, took his seat by her side. They had not proceeded very far when a brougham passed, and Cora started when she saw the occupant was Sir Reginald, but so engrossed was he, that he never noticed her.

"Now, Cora," said Percy, "I will tell you how I found out where you were. Thanks be to God that I was the means of saving you from the hands of that villain. I called at your house this afternoon, with a message from Miss Earl, who was very anxious to see you. Your mother informed me that you had just left for the purpose of seeing your friend, and more, she added, 'the carriage came for her.' I thought it strange, but said nothing, fearing to alarm her. I hurried back to Park Lane, and asked for you. Both my cousin and Miss Earl were lost in amazement when I told them that a carriage had been sent to fetch you in their name. I rushed back, and found your mother in a great state of uneasiness at your non-appearance. 'This is the letter she received, requesting her to go,' she said, placing the forgery in my hands, 'and a most respectable-looking old man-servant accompanied the carriage,' she added. Then for the first time the thought flashed across my mind that you had fallen into the hands of Captain Lance or my cousin Reginald. Bidding your mother compose herself, for that I would endeavour to bring you back, I started for Reginald's rooms. He was away, his servant told me, with Captain Lance, and he would not return that night. I went to Lance's, and met with the same reply. I was almost in despair when a man touched me on the arm ; I turned round, thinking it was some mendicant asking alms, but was surprised to see a respectably dressed man. 'Your pardon, sir,' he said, 'but can I be of any use?' Seeing my look of astonishment, he continued, 'are you not desirous of knowing where the gentleman who lives there is gone?' 'Yes, I am.' 'Then I can tell you, and more, I can also tell you where the servant of that man has taken a young lady this afternoon.' I took his arm. 'Is it possible?' I asked ; 'but how do you know these things?' 'That's my business, sir, but if you like to pay me for my news, say so, and I will tell you where to find her.'

"How quickly I complied, I need not say, and he then told me that having occasion for some reason of his own

to watch the servant of Captain Lance, he also watched
the master, and seeing the servant leave with his master's
brougham, he followed ; saw him go to your house, and
drive away with you in it.   He still followed, and was
astonished to see you driven to that house at Battersea,
and the brougham return empty.   Knowing the character
of the man he was watching, he determined to unravel
the mystery, and chance favoured him in seeing me leave
Captain Lance's house in a state of great excitement.
The idea struck him that your disappearance might have
something to do with it : hence his reason for accosting
me.   'And now, sir, if you like, I will show you where
the lady is,' he said ; ' you will have an hour's start of
them if you go at once, for I heard that precious scoundrel order the brougham at ten, and it is now but nine.'
We called a cab, and arrived at the house where you
were imprisoned.   My unknown friend accompanied
me.   The only person in the house was the woman, and
she asked no questions, evidently taking me for one of
her employers, but pointed upstairs to the room in which
you were.   When you and I came down stairs, the door
was open, as you know, and both the woman and my
strange friend were gone.   And now I have told you
all.''

Cora's tears were falling fast during this recital.
Now that all danger was past, her over-taxed strength
gave way, and though she struggled to retain her composure, it was in vain ; Nature would have her own way
for once.

"We are nearly at your home, Miss Wilton.   I pray
you bear up for the sake of your mother, whose anxiety
on your account must be fearful by this time," Percy
urged.

"Miss Wilton, how cold and studied his manner is,"
thought Cora ; "quite changed!   In that house he called
me Cora.   What can it mean ?   Perhaps he is ashamed
of loving an actress ; but he will see I can be as proud
as he."

So she dried her tears.   When they arrived at her
house, Percy excused himself from entering.   Cora bade

him good night, and though she thanked him for the great service he had rendered her, not a note in her voice trembled. Poor Cora, she had learnt to control her voice, though not her feelings, and well for her it was dark, or the tell-tale blushes would have revealed what she so bravely strove to conceal. The door closed on her, and Percy was alone.

"She thanks me coldly and proudly," he moaned. "Could she but see how my heart is breaking in its efforts to tear her image from it, she would pity me ; but it is better as it is—far better she should think me cold and heartless than that I should forfeit my honour. I have rescued her from a fate far worse than death, and the remembrance of that will help me to perform my duty."

Here Percy's meditations were interrupted by his arrival at his own rooms.

CHAPTER XIV

A TERRIBLE ACCUSATION.

WE left Ella by her mother's bedside, in a wretched lodging in Camden Town. We see her again in a beautiful boudoir in the house in Park Lane on the night of Cora's abduction. Poor Eva's trials are over ; she sleeps the sleep that knows no waking. Like a tired child, she sank to rest in the arms of her husband, happy and contented. Mr. Earl mourned deeply for her, but a great weight was lifted from his heart ; she had died blessing him, and he could henceforward mourn her as the dear wife he would meet again. Besides, he had his children to live for. He had adopted Eunice as his own, and the sad, silent-looking child, so like her mother, appealed to his heart, even, perhaps, more than Ella.

After his wife's death, Maud invited Ella and Eunice to Park Lane, where they were now staying, until the establishment Mr. Earl had taken should be ready to receive them. Ella and Maud became fast friends, and though no two natures could be more dissimilar than the patrician lady's and the *ci-devant* ballet-girl's, their friendship was a true one, founded on respect. Maud, with her warm, affectionate nature, had taken Ella to her heart, and loved her truly, in spite of her silent, reserved manner ; while Ella's love for the beautiful, bright being who had given her her friendship, almost bordered on adoration. Little Eunice, since her mother's death, would never be parted from Mr. Earl ; it seemed as though the child had transferred all the love she had for her mother to him, and he returned it tenfold, petting and doing his best to spoil her.

Ella had not altered much, save that she looked paler in her black dress, and the expression of anxiety which was wont to be on her countenance had disappeared. She mourned her mother sincerely ; but the dreadful doubt that would intrude on her mind as to whether that mother was entitled to her respect was banished for ever ; and in the society of her father, sister, and Maud she was very happy.

Yet something seemed to have occurred to agitate her this evening.

"Past ten," she exclaimed, as a beautiful ormolu and gold time-piece struck the hour, "and no news of Cora ! who can have sent for her in my name ? but perhaps Mr. Lysle is in the drawing-room, with news ; I will go and see."

But a knock at the door, and the entrance of Maud prevented this.

"I have just come in, Ella, to tell you that Percy has not returned, and that uncle says, if you like he will go and see if he can gain any news of your friend Cora for you."

"No, darling, it is of no use, I fear, but come and sit with me, Maud ; I cannot enjoy this pretty room you have given me without your sweet society."

"Very well, Ella, I will stay ; I should have come, but thought, perhaps, you would prefer being alone, but tell me about this Cora ; I remember seeing her two years ago at Elmerton. She is very, very pretty, and do you know I should like to know her, for, from all you have told me about her, I am sure she must be a sweet girl."

" Ah, dear, your position is so different to Cora's. What would the world say to the beautiful, high-born Maud Clayton associating with the actress, Cora Wilton ? No, dear, that must not be."

" But, Ella, when I am married, the world you fear so much can say nothing, and you know, dear, that I am to be Maud Clayton but a few weeks longer," she added, with a blush, " and oh, Ella, I am so happy !"

Throwing herself into her friend's arms, she continued, " Dear Percy loves me, and I should die without his love—I know I should. For some time before uncle found you, I thought I should have to part from Percy, and indeed, Ella, I nearly died that night, although no one knew anything about it. I do not think, Ella, that I shall live very long, though I should like to for Percy's sake ; but I am like mamma, and she died when she was very young, and my grandmamma also, and I have a kind of presentiment that something dreadful is going to happen to me. We Earls are a very short-lived family ; there is only Uncle Walter, you see, Ella, and he has the strength of all."

" But, darling, you are a Clayton, I am an Earl, and according to your theory, I shall not live very long. But, Maud, sweet one, you must get these fancies out of your pretty little head. What should I do without my loved cousin ? And poor papa would break his heart, and a certain young gentleman I know would be very, very cross did he hear you give way to such gloomy forbodings. No, Maud, you will live to laugh at these thoughts ; and now, dearest, as you look tired, let me go with you and help you to undress, instead of your maid."

The two girls retired to Maud's room, the one to fall into a sweet sleep, and the other to watch over her for hours. Ella had got into the habit of late hours, and do all she would, she could not sleep until after midnight, so she generally remained with Maud, reading her to sleep or talking with her, until she felt inclined to woo

9

the drowsy god on her own account. This night, after
Maud had gone to sleep, Ella felt restless, and could not
shake off the impression that Maud's words had made
on her. It was long after the whole household were
quiet, that she took her light and passed into her own
room, which adjoined Maud's, but then she could not
sleep, and the morning light found her still awake.

Percy Lysle was sitting at breakfast the morning after
his rescue of Cora, when his servant entered and announced that two persons were very desirous of speaking
to Mr. Lysle on a matter of great importance.

"Who are they, James?" asked Percy. "Have you
seen them before?"

"No, sir; they look very much like detectives."

"What can they want, I wonder? But show them
in."

The servant bowed and withdrew, and in a few moments the two men entered. One was a middle-aged,
good-tempered looking man, but the other was tall and
thin, with light grey eyes, with a sharp penetrating expression, and directly he entered Percy had the uncomfortable feeling that he was being looked through.

When James had left the room, the elder, who introduced himself as Mr. Stock, closed the door and bolted
it. Noticing Percy's look of astonishment at such a
proceeding, he remarked that it was always best to be on
your guard against interruption. For a moment Percy
thought that the men who were now in the room meant
to rob him, but a second's consideration was sufficient to
banish that idea, and he awaited in silence for them to
explain the object of their visit.

After a pause, the good-tempered looking man commenced the conversation by remarking that this was a
strange business.

"What is a strange business?" said Percy, completely
mystified.

"Why, this murder last night."

"Murder! But what has any murder to do with your
visit to me?"

"Only that you being one of the gentleman's relations,

and being last seen in his company, are supposed to know something about it, that's all."

"I don't quite understand you; you say that there has been a murder, and that I was in the murdered person's company, but you don't tell me who the person was. Perhaps, my good friends, you will be kind enough to explain, while I finish my breakfast."

"Well! you are a cool hand," said the short man; "but, Smith, you tell the gentleman all about it."

"Well, sir, you see that Sir Reginald Clayton was murdered last night."

"Reginald murdered!" exclaimed Percy, and all the cool manner disappeared as if by magic at the dreadful news, "who by?"

"Ah, that, sir, is what we want to arrive at. So perhaps you will not mind putting on your things and accompanying us," was the quiet rejoinder.

"Of course, I will," said Percy, "but what did you mean by saying just now that I was the last person seen with him? I have not seen him to speak to for three weeks or more."

"Well, sir, if you can prove that before the magistrate it will be all right."

"What," said Percy, as the truth dawned upon him, "you surely do not suspect me of the murder? Oh God! this is too awful. But tell me how this happened, and by what hideous mockery the commission of this fearful crime is supposed to fall on me?"

"Well, sir, if you will come with us you will know all about it, but in the meantime let's caution you that anything you may say will be taken in evidence against you."

Percy rang the bell for his servant, and telling him he was going out with these gentlemen, bade him call a cab, and was soon on his way to the Police Station.

The magistrate happened to be a personal friend of Percy's, and said to him when he entered, "This is a very sad affair, Mr. Lysle," in a cold constrained voice, "a very sad affair."

"Will you have the kindness to tell me what it all

means," said Percy, " for at present I am in the dark,
and know not if I am awake or in a fearful dream from
which I shall soon be startled."

"Alas! Mr. Lysle, it is all real, and you stand in a
very critical position.   Your cousin, Sir Reginald Clayton, with whom it appears you have been on extremely
bad terms for some weeks, was found murdered, and a
witness comes forward to prove that you were the last
person in his company, and that he heard high words
pass between you."

"I assure you I have not seen my late cousin to speak
to him for some weeks, neither did we ever have any
serious quarrel," was his quiet answer.

"Can you bring any witness to prove that you were
not at Helsdon House, Battersea, last night?"

"No.   I can bring no witness to prove that, for I was
there, but I can bring one forward who was with me
all the time, to prove that Sir Reginald was not on the
premises during the while I remained there, which was
very short, but I decline calling this witness."

"Mr. Lysle, this is madness.   Do you not know that
in the absence of any evidence in your favour, I shall be
compelled to commit you for trial."

"I am perfectly aware of that fact, sir, but still shall
not call the witness in question."

And Percy Lysle was committed to take his trial for
the wilful murder of his cousin, Sir Reginald Clayton.
As he was conducted to prison the horror and danger of
his position dawned upon him.   He had been too excited
all the morning to give much thought to the danger;
indeed he had imagined it impossible so monstrous an
accusation could be believed against him, but upon the
evidence he had heard, upon reflection he could not but
acknowledge he was in an extremely awkward position.
When the prison was reached, the Governor received
him, and having heard the case, lodged Percy in his own
house.   Nevertheless he was a prisoner to all intents and
purposes on a charge of murder.   The first feeling of
degradation and shame over, he saw it was no time for
delay, and that action alone could help him.   Accord-

ingly he at once sent for his solicitor. Mr. Edgar was the senior partner of one of the most respectable and old established firms in the city ; they had been from time immemorial the legal advisers of the Lysles, so to him Percy naturally turned for advice and help. Mr. Edgar was extremely surprised at receiving a summons from one of his best clients directed from the Old Bailey. He wasted but little time in conjectures, and a very short period saw him on his way to the prison.

Percy was pacing the room with impatient steps when Mr. Edgar entered.

" Thank God, you have come at last," he exclaimed, as he grasped the old lawyer's hand. " Minutes seem like hours in this place."

" But, my dear boy—Mr Lysle, I mean—what is all this ? Why do I find you here ?"

" In the first place call me Percy, as you used to do in the years gone by ; you, as the old and valued friend of my father, have the right, and let me not think that you can entertain the slightest suspicion that I am in any way guilty of the fearful crime with which I am charged by coldly calling me Mr. Lysle."

" Fearful crime that you are charged with ! What does it all mean ? Am I the victim of a delusion ! Explain, I implore you, Percy, before I become thoroughly confused."

" I will do so. Listen, I am accused of the murder of my cousin, Sir Reginald Clayton."

At the words Mr. Edgar sprang from his chair perfectly electrified, but in a moment recovered his composure, and attended to Percy's story. at the close of which he was silent for a few seconds, and then asked abruptly if he took the cabman's number ?

" No," replied Percy, "but I should know the man who drove, if I were to see him anywhere, for I remember remarking to myself what a singular looking face his was."

" Can you describe him ?"

" Yes, he was middle-aged, short and muscular in figure, but with a face in which no two features seemed

to correspond; his eyes looked different ways, his nose
was sharp and hooked like a bird's beak, and his mouth
was large, with thick lips and projecting teeth. He had
on an old white hat with a black band, and a very much
worn grey overcoat, many sizes too large for him."

"That will do for him, and now for the other man
who met you outside Captain Lance's chambers, and accompanied you to Battersea."

"It was dark, and he kept his face hidden from me as
much as possible; but the occasional glimpses I caught
of his features as we passed the street lamps impressed
me with the idea that it was not at all an English face."

"Can you give me no further description?" interro-
gated Mr. Edgar.

"No, but if I heard his voice I should recognise it."

"Well, the first thing to be done is to find the
cabman who drove you, and by that and Miss Wilton's
evidence prove an alibi, and afterwards discover the real
murderer."

"But Mr. Edgar, we must do without Miss Wilton's
evidence: she must not be dragged into this miserable
case, and badgered and brow-beaten by the counsel for
the prosecution."

"Percy, this is madness; her evidence is of the first
importance."

"No matter, I would rather die than her name should
be bandied about in a court of justice in a case of
murder."

"But, Percy, what has she to fear? You saved her
from a wretched fate, and will it impose more on her
than the inconvenience and trouble it is her duty to
take, after what you have done for her? besides, she is
used to the public gaze; and what would be death to a
timid, gentle nature, will only be excitement to her,"
said the old man, with a half sneer, for he had no great
opinion of actresses generally, and poor Cora he positively disliked, although he had never even seen her, as
he considered her the indirect cause of his young friend's
trouble.

"If you wish not to offend me, Mr. Edgar, you will

speak less lightly of Miss Wilton. She is as pure as an
angel," said Percy, his face aglow with indignation at
the sneering way in which Mr. Edgar had spoken of her.

"Forgive me, Percy, if I have wounded you by my
remarks. I have no wish to speak disparagingly of the
young lady, of whom I know nothing, but," he added
gravely, "I am grieved to see you taking up the cudgels
in her defence so warmly. What can there be in common between an actress, no matter how beautiful and
good, and you, the last descendant of an old and proud
family? However, you are on the eve of marriage with
Miss Clayton. Be warned in time! Forgive me for
thus speaking to you, but remember that I, as an old
friend of your father's, have the right to speak to and
advise his son. But now I must leave you, and see what
can be done to release you from this horrible position.
Keep up your spirits, and rest assured what can be
shall be done, and that quickly. And now farewell for
the present."

Mr. Edgar had not left long when Percy had a visit
from Mr. Earl. He shook hands warmly with his
nephew, and that action took a weight of anxiety off the
poor fellow's heart, for he saw at once that he was
another friend, and did not suspect him of guilt.
Walter Earl was greatly agitated, and it was some few
moments before he could find strength to speak.

"Maud!" exclaimed Percy, "does she know anything
of this fearful tragedy?"

"No, not as yet, and I trust we may be able to keep
it from her; I only heard of it just now, and hurried to
you at once, my poor boy. How did it happen, tell me?
Except that Reginald is dead, and that you are in some
way connected with it, I am perfectly ignorant."

"Alas! I know little more than you, but what I do,
I will tell you." And Percy repeated the information
already know to the reader.

"But, Percy, why did you not come to us last night?"

"Because it was so late, therefore I went home."

"Your valet can prove what time you were at home."

"Alas! no, for I had given him permission to visit

some of his friends who live in the country, and he cannot return until to-day, and all the other servants had
gone to bed when I returned. So I let myself in by my
latch-key. I have seen Mr. Edgar, and the most important thing is to find the cabman who drove us, and
the man I met outside Captain Lance's chambers."

"But Miss Wilton is a most important witness; let
me call on her and tell her the fearful crime with which
you are charged through helping her, and rest assured
she will come forward to your assistance. Besides she
owes it to you as well as to herself, and she will be less
than a woman if she does not put aside pride and self in
a case like this."

Percy at last gave an unwilling consent to his
uncle's repeated entreaties, and Mr. Earl left him.

* * * * *

Cora was sitting at work when Mr. Earl was announced. "And if you please, Miss," said the servant,
"the gentleman bade me tell you it was a matter of life
and death, so he hoped you could see him quickly."
Cora threw down her work, and without further delay
entered the little drawing-room. Walter Earl awaited
her. He was struck by her appearance, and saw his
task, as far as she was concerned, would be an easy one.

"I make your acquaintance, Miss Wilton," he began,
"under very painful circumstances. You were last
night, I believe, rescued from a rather perilous position
by Mr. Lysle, were you not?"

"Indeed I was, and deeply grateful I shall ever be to
him for it."

"I was sure that was the case, and you would not
shrink from a disagreeable ordeal to prove that gratitude, would you?"

"Certainly not; if by so doing I could be of any
service to him."

"Then Miss Wilton, the case is this: Reginald Clayton, into whose hands you were so nearly falling, was
murdered last night,—but heavens! what is the matter?"
said Mr. Earl, as poor Cora fell from her chair at the

sad news, so suddenly broken to her. "Fool that I am. Perhaps the poor girl was attached to Reginald after all, and I have killed her. No, thank God, she breathes," for Cora gave signs of returning life. "I had better ring for assistance, and yet she may not wish it known; no, I will wait, as she seems to be getting better."

He took some water which was in a jug on the side-table, and bathed her forehead, and in a few moments had the satisfaction of seeing her open her eyes. As soon as she recovered sufficient strength, she signed to Mr. Earl to proceed with his story. He then informed her, though with more caution, that Percy was taken up on suspicion of the murder.

"And now you see, Miss Wilton, how you can help us. You are a most important witness in his favour, for you can prove that he was with you last night at past ten o'clock, and although it does not clear him completely, it will be greatly in his favour."

"I see, sir, and you may depend upon my giving all the assistance in my power to my preserver, but I feel so unwell just now that I must beg you to leave me."

"Thank you, Miss Wilton, and forgive me for breaking the sad news so abruptly, but in my grief and excitement, I hardly knew what I did."

After he had left, Cora could scarcely realize what she had just heard, and she rubbed her eyes, hoping that she would awake to find it all a horrid nightmare. "Reginald murdered, and Mr. Lysle accused of the crime! it cannot be true," she cried. "I shall go mad, and all my own doing. But for my deception two years ago all this might have been averted. Oh! how Percy Lysle will despise me when he hears the truth, and father and mother will be deeply wounded, perhaps never trust me again. What shall I do? I have no courage to tell mamma now, and see the look of pain on her dear face as she listens to the tale of deception practised on her by her only child, whom she thought so truthful and honest. But I must tell her; it will be better for her to hear it from me than in the court, where it is sure to be discovered." On this determination our heroine persisted, and while we are leaving her to unburden her mind to her mother, let us see what is going on in another part of the great Metropolis.

CHAPTER XV

ON THE TRACK.

ON the early morning of the day in which the events recorded in the last chapter took place, a man so muffled up that it was impossible to recognise him, was walking very briskly down Whitechapel Road, and after looking anxiously round to see if he was followed, he dived down one of the numerous courts that abound in that populous and squalid neighbourhood. He walked some way along the alley until he came to a tall, old house, black with dirt and age. It was all closed up, but the man knocked twice on the shutter, and after a few moments' delay, the door was noiselessly opened for his entrance, and as noiselessly shut again. The man groped his way along a dark passage towards a glimmer of light which shone from under a door, and turning the handle, entered.

Three men occupied the room, which was small, and seemingly without any outlet, save the door-way through which the man had entered. The men all rose at his appearance, and it was plain to see they were men under the ban of the law and of society, by the fear and alarm depicted on their faces at the abrupt entrance of the stranger.

"Sit down," said the man, with a laugh; "you don't take me for a 'peeler,' do you?" And he took a chair and proceeded to divest himself of the clothes that had so completely disguised him.

"Why," said one of the men, "if it's not Cross-eyed Bill, I declare. Well, what are you about?"

"All in good time; don't be in a hurry, but first give a taste of something warm to a fellow, for I've had a

night's work, I can tell you." Saying this he drew
near the fire-place to warm his hands, while one of the
men poured out some gin from a bottle which stood on
the table into a mug, and handed it to him. Without
his wraps, he was a singular-looking man enough, rather
below the middle height, broad and muscular, with a
large head, and eyes that looked different ways ; a nose,
thin and hooked, like a bird of prey, added to a large
mouth with thick lips and projecting teeth, made up an
appearance far from prepossessing. The other occupants of the room were of the usual type of the English
rough, bullet-headed, thick-necked, sensual-looking
animals, but without the ferocious expression there was
in the eyes of the new comer.

"Well, lads, now I am a little warm I'll tell you all
about what I've done. You know I've been hunting for
that Joe ever since we managed to escape from across
the herring-pond, where he sent us for his own work ;
and you remember I told him I'd be even with him some
day. Well, I've found him, and for some time have
been dogging him about. Last night I'd been waiting
for him when a young gent comes up with a lady, and
asks me to take 'em in the cab, which I does, but after
taking the gent home I returns to the house I was
watching, because I had an idea that something was
up. Well, when I gets back it was late. I sees a light
in the empty house, so, tying the 'oss up where no one
would see it, I went down to the house, found the gate
unlocked, got into the court, and climbed up to the
winder where the light was burning. I looked in and
saw Joe and a holder man, like a furriner, standing over
a gent, who it was plain to see they was making away
with. I should ha' tried to 'elp him, but I see at once
he was past 'elp, and I didn't care to risk my life with
two to one against me ; so I jist kep quiet, and seed 'em
pick his pockets and leave. A stick was in Joe's hand
with blood on it, and a pistol was on the floor. They
left the house, locking the door. I got back to the cab
and oss, and druv away. Now in a day or two a large
reward will be offered for the murderer, and I can come

forward and get it, and pay back Joe without putting
my own neck in danger. What do you say, pals? Will
that suit your books? We can divide the swag amongst
us. Now, having that settled, I'll take a nap, for I feel
precious tired."

So saying, he stretched himself before the fire, and in
a few minutes was fast asleep.

＊　　　　＊　　　　＊　　　　＊　　　　＊

When Mr. Earl reached Park Lane after the exciting
events of the day, he found he had not left sorrow and
care behind him, for there awaited him trouble even
more overwhelming. Maud, the good and beautiful,
was dying! The news of her brother's murder and
Percy's arrest had been abruptly told her by her
frightened maid, and the excitement and distress had
caused the rupture of a blood vessel on the lungs.

"Is there no hope?" asked Mr. Earl of the physician
who had been called in conjunction with the family
doctor.

"No, sir; I regret to say that it is impossible that
Miss Clayton can recover. She may possibly linger
some few weeks, but the shock her system has received,
added to the loss of blood she has sustained, precludes
all hope of a permanent recovery."

Mr. Earl was so stupefied at the suddenness of the
blow that it was some time before he could realize the fact
that Maud, so full of life and love but a few short hours
ago, was now awaiting the approach of death.

"Can I see her?" he asked; "I promise to be perfectly calm in her presence. Only let me see her."

The physician assented, and himself conducted Mr.
Earl to the couch on which she was lying in her little
morning room, where she had heard the fearful news
that had given her her death-blow. The doctor had
desired she might remain where she was, as any attempt
to move her would hasten the end.

When Mr. Earl entered and saw her lying like a
broken lily among her birds and flowers, where he had
seen her so often blithe and happy, his fortitude nearly
gave way; but, by a strong effort, he recovered himself,

and approached Maud. She was conscious, and greeted him with a look of eager inquiry, which almost broke his heart, as he thought of the little comfort he could really give. But a sign from Ella, who was holding her cousin's head, reminded him that truth must be sacrificed, and he whispered that all would be right.

"And, Percy?" ejaculated the dying girl, in a husky voice.

"Hush, dear; do not speak," said Ella, as her handkerchief was stained after the effort, "and papa will tell you all."

The task was an awful one for Walter Earl, though he glossed over the dreadful facts as well as he could. Maud's tears fell fast during the recital, and several times he left off; but the anxiety the poor girl evinced to know all was far more dangerous, the doctor said, than if the truth were told her, so he had to resume his tale of horror. At last it was finished, and Walter Earl felt that the severest ordeal of his life had been passed through. In the short time the recital had taken, he seemed to have lived years of agony, and every expression of pain that passed over his niece's face, found an echo in his heart.

"Now, darling," he said in conclusion, "try and bear up for our sakes. Trust in Providence, which alone can help us."

The doctors saw that the excitement Maud was undergoing might bring on another attack of hæmorrhage, and therefore signed to Mr. Earl to leave the room.

He passed the night in the library. Sleep became out of the question in the state of mind from which he suffered; he longed for the morning, that he might be doing something to relieve the agony he was enduring, but the hours passed on leaden wings. At last a ray of sunshine appeared. Maud had dropped into a calm sleep, and was still sleeping when Mr. Earl left the house to try and discover the murderer of his nephew, Reginald.

He first went to Scotland Yard, where he had an interview with one of the most shrewd detectives, named Cole, which lasted some time. They both went together to the Old Bailey, and had a conversation with Percy relative to the case in question, and the detective left with the assurance that what could be done by mortal man to unravel the mystery, should be done.

"We have but a week to the trial," said the detective, "but don't despair, sir; once on the track, and I will find the guilty parties if they are above ground; but the first thing is to offer a reward for information, and if it be large enough, I warrant we shall hear something before this time to-morrow."

But in spite of this assurance, day after day passed and still no news, until the evening before the trial had arrived. Mr. Earl had spent nearly the whole of the day with Percy, but had not found courage to tell him of Maud's state, although she, to the surprise of all, rallied, and still lingered on. It was on this evening he was leaving the prison when a man touched him on the shoulder. Turning round he saw a poor workman.

"Don't you know me, sir?" he asked.

"Why!" he exclaimed in astonishment, "it is Mr. Cole."

"Hush, sir, for God's sake, only one word. Got news—all right."

And without further parley he walked away swiftly, leaving Walter Earl in a state of complete bewilderment.

CHAPTER XVI.

THE TRIAL FOR MURDER.

THE morning of the eventful day on the which Percy Lysle was to be tried for the murder of his cousin, was ushered in with a terrific storm of rain and wind, yet in spite of the war waged by the elements, the court was densely crowded at an early hour, so great was the interest excited in the Metropolis by the murder of Sir Reginald Clayton, and the anxiety to catch a glimpse of the supposed murderer. Many and absurd were the

garbled accounts put forth by the sensational news-
papers; and the news of Maud's state, which, in spite
of all precautions, had become known, threw an air of
romance over the whole affair, for which the sensational
and horror-loving portion of the public were truly
grateful. Percy was calm and collected as he entered
the dock, and a murmur ran through the crowd of human
beings, his appearance, youth, and good looks and un-
flinching demeanour having evidently created an impression in his favour; and when, in answer to the charge,
he pleaded Not Guilty, in a firm, distinct voice, something very like a cheer arose. This was quickly sup-
pressed, and the case for the prosecution was opened.

The first witness called was Percy's valet. After a
long examination he was dismissed from the witness-box,
having really nothing to tell. After him came Sir
Reginald's man servant, Adolphe. The man got into
the witness-box, and was duly sworn.

"Your name is Adolphe Debeson, is it not, and you
are a native of France?" So the counsel for the prosecution began.

"Stay one moment," said Percy's counsel, getting up,
"will you permit me to put a question to this witness?"

Permission was granted, and he turned to Adolphe and
asked him in slow, distinct accents:—

"Were you never known by any other name?"

There was little in the question to cause such emotion,
but the man's face became convulsed with fear, and he
was so overcome that he could not give his evidence, and
had to stand down. The next witness for the prosecution was called, and Joseph White stepped forth.

He deposed to first seeing the accused with Sir Reginald Clayton, about two months before at his master's,
Captain Lance, in the Albany; they seemed at that
time on good terms. Saw him again a week later; they
were playing cards, and thought Mr. Lysle lost; for
when he entered the room with refreshments, Mr. Lysle
looked agitated and troubled. Heard high words
between Sir Reginald and Mr. Lysle, and distinctly
heard Mr. Lysle say he would have his revenge. Did

not see Mr. Lysle again, until the night of the murder.
Sir Reginald was in love with a lady, an actress ; and
had appointed to meet her at Helsdon House, Battersea.
Drove Sir Reginald himself down to the house in his
master's brougham, and was dismissed by Sir Reginald
at the top of the lane, with directions to return in two
hours for him. As he was driving away, saw the accused
turn down the lane and follow Sir Reginald. Could
swear it was him. Felt sure something was up, because
he knew Mr. Lysle was in love with the same lady.
Heard Sir Reginald tell his master so, and boast how he
would win her in spite of his cousin. The lady went
willingly to meet Sir Reginald, because he, Joseph White,
took the note from Sir Reginald to the lady's house,
and she came down, and he drove her to Helsdon House.
It was about four in the afternoon. Sir Reginald did
not go until ten o'clock. Felt so certain something was
up, that he would not stay away more than half-an-hour ;
and when about a hundred yards from the top of the lane
leading to the house, saw a man coming along the road,
and walking very fast as he passed. Noticed by the light
of the carriage-lamp that it was Mr. Lysle, and that he
was very pale and agitated. Waited two hours for Sir
Reginald ; and, as he did not come, began to fear
something was the matter. Heard a clock strike one, so
thought it was time to go and see ; but was afraid to go
alone—besides, he could not leave the carriage. Drove
some distance up the road, and met two policemen.
Told them that he was waiting for a gentleman, and that
he was so long past the time he told him to come that
he was afraid something was the matter, and asked if
they would mind going to see, as he could not leave his
horse ? They said it was a rum rig, a gentleman going
to Helsdon House : but, perhaps, he wanted to see the
ghost. Said he thought it was very likely, because he
did not like to say there was a lady in the case ; for Sir
Reginald was an awful temper, and thought after all he
might only be a little late. The policeman went, but returned
in about a quarter of an hour, saying that the gentleman
was murdered. In the fear of the moment, at hearing

such an awful thing, said, "Ah! Then Mr. Lysle has done it." Went with the policeman to a magistrate and told all he had just said.

"Captain Algernon Lance," called the crier. And Captain Lance took his place in the witness-box, vacated by his precious servant. Percy was perfectly bewildered by the perjury of the last witness. Yet still he wondered what Captain Lance could say against him. "I have never done him any harm," thought the poor fellow; but he had yet to learn that it is not necessary to wrong a bad man to make him your bitter enemy

Captain Lance began giving his evidence in a low, reluctant voice, as though it really caused him pain.

"You know the prisoner?" asked the counsel for the prosecution.

"Yes," replied Lance, with a sigh.

"And you were a particular friend of the deceased, Sir Reginald Clayton?"

Captain Lance's feelings so overcame him at this question, that it was some moments before he could reply. His sensibility had its effect for many there, and murmurs of approbation greeted his ear. At length, having overcome the extreme anguish of his feelings, he went on with his evidence.

"Can you give an account of Sir Reginald Clayton, last night?" asked the counsel, and Lance replied he would tell all he knew. His poor friend, he knew, was deeply enamoured of an actress, who, so far as he understood, returned in some measure his passion at one time; but Mr. Lysle also admired this lady, and Sir Reginald had told him that her preference for him had almost driven Mr. Lysle mad. He knew Sir Reginald was to meet her the night when he met with his death, but whether by appointment or otherwise he did not enquire, as it was no business of his. He lent his brougham, as he himself was out of town and did not require it. Believed Mr. Lysle was a very violent tempered man. Had always heard such was the case, and remembered his poor murdered friend telling him of the fact. Really could not say anything more, save his own impressions,

10

and those if not favourable to persons, he always made a rule of keeping to himself. Such being the case must decline speaking further.

With Algernon Lance the evidence for the prosecution closed. Percy was as one in a dream. That he should for one moment be thought guilty of such a crime was very sad and trouble enough ; but the evidence he had just heard was sufficient to condemn him. How should he get out of this fearful mesh that was closing around him ! Stay, there was a stir in the court, as Miss Cora Wilton, the first witness for the defence, was called. Percy leant forward. Was it fancy, or did Captain Lance really change colour as Cora, calm and pale, came forward in answer to her name? Every voice was hushed and every eye directed on the public favourite. "She then is the actress who is the cause of all this," people murmured. As Cora related her story the impress that truth always makes was deeply felt. She began from her first acquaintance years before with the murdered man : her love for him, and his vile proposals, and her rejection of them. She glossed over nothing, and then went on to tell of her struggle to forget him,—her victory over herself, and how when she again met him her heart was only full of scorn and detestation for him. She related the offer of his hand made to her and her rejection of him,— his vow to be revenged upon her. In fact, she told all that the reader already knows ; but she could not say what happened after Mr. Lysle left her at her mother's house.

The counsel for the prosecution made a most able speech ; and thought there could be little doubt concerning the verdict. Just at this juncture, a slight commotion was noticed in the court, and a slip of paper was handed to Percy's solicitor, which he read, and immediately turning to the judge, prayed that he might bring forward a most important witness. Permission was granted, and Percy's counsel, getting up, exclaimed, "Let the door be closed ; for the real murderers are in court."

At these words a scream was heard, and Percy clutched the rail of the dock for support, as in the new witness he recognised the cabman who drove him home on the night of the murder. As he stepped into the witness-box a loud fall was heard, and it was found that Joseph White had fainted. After the commotion occasioned by this circumstance had subsided, the man was sworn.

"What is your name?" demanded the counsel for the prosecution.

"Ask your witness there," replied the man, with a leer; "he'll tell you; but as he is so overcome at seeing an old pal, I'll tell you myself. It's Bill Smith, but known better as 'Cross-eyed Bill.' Ah! Joe, how are you now?" said Smith, as that worthy, having recovered from his fainting-fit, resumed his place. "You see we have met again; I told you we should, and this time I can pay you back with interest. In the first place," turning to the judge, "the man who put the poor gent out of the world is my friend here, and I'll tell you all about it."

At these extraordinary words there was the greatest excitement manifested in the court; but, order being restored, Bill Smith resumed:

"If you please, may I tell my tale my own way?" he asked; and, his request being granted, he related as follows:—"Many years ago, I became acquainted with Joe White. He was a servant out of place, and married to a fellow-servant, whom he treated shamefully. After a time she died, and he was taken up for the murder. He got off; but, after that time, he was looked down upon like, and he soon jined a lot of us who was not very particular what we did; but we never had any blood to answer for until he jound us. One night we cracked a jeweller's in the city, and the old man himself, hearing the noise, came down. We was all for running, but Joe was for quieting the old man, saying, 'dead men told no tales.' We was all against it; but, just then, the old man set up a shriek, and Joe settled him without further ado. We was caught, and Joe turned evidence against us, and one of our pals was hanged for his work. Me

10—2

and another was transported; but I swore to be even with him, and now I can pay the debt. I worked hard, got my ticket of leave, and returned to England, for the purpose of paying off Joe. I got a cab, and turned cab-driver; for I had had enough of the other life, and determined not to return to it. One day I saw Joe White, and tracked him to the Albany, made enquiries, and found he was servant to a gent named Lance; I watched him always, because I knew he must be up to something; I saw him often with that Frenchman there; and, on the afternoon of the murder, had taken him to Helsdon House, Battersea. He did not know me, but I knew him well enough; and, my suspicions being aroused, in the evening I returned to watch the house, and see what was going on there. When I see that gent there, and a lady; he hailed me, and asked if I was engaged. I thought I might as well take a fare, so drove them to Adelina Terrace, Hyde Park, where the lady got out, and afterwards the gentleman went to Albemarle Street, Piccadilly. After that, I drove as fast as I could back, and tied my hoss up, went round the lane to Helsdon House; the gate was undone, and I went round to the back, looking over the river. I see a light in a window on the second floor, and climbed up by the ivy, which is all over the house, and looked in the window, and there I see a gentleman on the ground, and that Frenchman and Joe standing over him. Joe had a stick with blood on it, and a pistol was on the floor, and I see the gent was dead. I see Joe take a letter out of the gent's pocket, and also his purse; the Frenchman took nothing, but stood looking at the body, as though he was pleased to see him dead. I would have gone in, but I see the gent was quite gone, and I knew that I should be served the same if Joe saw me; so I got down, and waited in the lane, and see them come out, and drove as fast as I could back to London."

As the man finished his evidence a murmur ran through the court. Cross-examination failed to shake his evidence in the faintest degree, and so, without hesitation the jury returned a verdict of acquittal, and

Percy Lysle stepped from the dock amid the cheers of the people who filled the court. Adolphe and Joe White took the place of Percy, and the Frenchman seeing all was over, confessed his participation in the murder of his master. He had committed the crime in revenge for the death of his sister, which had been caused by Sir Reginald, and so far from feeling sorrow for the deed of blood, he gloried that he had at last fulfilled his oath of vengeance. He stated that he was the man who met Percy and told him where Cora was, thinking by that means to throw the appearance of guilt on him; and how well he succeeded the reader already knows. He also confessed that he had been watching his opportunity for years, and had almost despaired of accomplishing it, until he made the acquaintance of Joe White, who, for a considerable sum of money, agreed to join him, and it was from him that he gained information of Sir Reginald's movements.

When Adolphe had finished his confession, it was apparent he was labouring under great physical suffering, but a feeling of horror had filled the court when he suddenly fell and expired before he could be removed from the dock. The wretched man had provided himself with poison in case the evidence turned against him, and so had rushed into his Maker's presence unbidden. But let us not judge him too harshly, for he had no doubt brooded over his wrongs until they had warped his brain, driving him to madness. With regard to Joe White, he was condemned to the death which he richly deserved for his many crimes.

CHAPTER XVII.

LOVE'S TRIUMPHS.

WHEN Percy Lysle left the dock his hand was grasped by Mr. Earl, and then for the first time he heard of Maud's deplorable state. All thoughts of Cora were banished from his mind by the sad news, and he passed the poor girl in court without a sign of recognition. Poor Cora! now all seemed dark indeed in the future to her. But we must leave her for awhile to follow Percy. As one in a dream he accompanied Mr. Earl. The events of the last two weeks seemed like some nightmare, from which he must awake. Maud dying! The words rang in his ear, and he thought, with an agony of remorse how cruel and faithless he had been to that pure, guileless heart. Gladly would he now have laid down his life could he by its sacrifice save Maud; but it was not to be. The fiat had gone forth, and Maud Clayton would soon be among the things of the past.

When they reached Park Lane, Ella, with her eyes red with weeping, met them, and pressed Percy's hand in silence.

It was not a time for congratulations, for Maud was sinking fast. Percy hurried to the room, praying that he might be in time to take leave of, and obtain forgiveness of his cousin. As he entered Maud was lying back exhausted with an attack of coughing, and he almost feared that the spirit had fled, but it was not so. Maud opened her eyes, and when they encountered Percy's a ray of joy passed over the features of the dying girl, and she held out her arms to him. Percy took her in his, and as the fair head rested upon his shoulder a flood of recollections rushed through his memory. He recalled the first time he had seen that girlish form replete with health and beauty. The memory of the night when she had confessed her pure love, and promised to be his wife came over him; he thought of all the trusting love she had given him, and the falsehood and cruelty with which he had repaid it, and now it was too late to atone, for she was dying. Yes! And he the principle cause of her death. In that moment all Maud's wrongs were avenged. He hated and despised himself with all the intensity of which his susceptible nature was capable.

After a time Maud regained strength enough to speak; but it was apparent enough to all that this was the final scene, in which Maud played a part in the great drama of life. We will pass over what followed, there is something too holy and sacred in a deathbed scene like Maud's to be spoken of here. Before the morning dawned her pure spirit had fled to the arms of her Saviour, and all that remained of sweet Maud Clayton was a calm, still, lovely image of clay. Those lips would smile no more, and those sunny eyes would never unclose again to lighten the sorrows of those around her. She had gone where only spirits like hers can go; she had joined her mother in the spirit land—that mother who had been the guardian angel of her pure young life.

It was some time before Percy could believe that she was dead, so calmly had she passed away; but when the truth could be no longer doubted, then came that dead feeling of agony that those only who have watched by the bedside of a dear lost one have felt when all is over. The sun shone, but it appeared to Percy a mockery, when one so bright had passed away.

The grief of Walter Earl was great, but he had his children to console him; and the remembrance of all the love and care he had lavished on his niece could not be otherwise than a source of comfort to him. When the will was opened, it was found that Maud who, by the death of Sir Reginald, had inherited all the estates, had bequeathed the bulk of her large fortune to Percy. But she had not forgotten her cousin Ella or little Eunice. To each of them she had left ten thousand pounds; and to Cora, whom she had but too much reason to hate, the sum of three thousand pounds. This, with a few legacies to her maid servants, completed the distribution of her property, and the race of Clayton became extinct.

Maud was the last of this line, and with her ended the
curse of Marion.

When Percy found this further proof of the dead girl's
love and devotion, his sufferings were even greater, and
the thought of Cora, who had unwittingly been the principal cause of his faithlessness to Maud, was hateful to
him—so often do we unjustly blame others for our own
faults. He added another two thousand pounds to the
legacy left by Maud, but in the deceased girl's name, for
he knew enough of Cora to know that she would accept
nothing from him, and then made arrangements to leave
England, without seeing the innocent cause of his
remorse. Although he strove to hide it from himself,
he loved Cora still, but the thought of an union with her
seemed desecration with that newly made grave between
them, so in a few weeks he bade adieu to England, hoping
in other climes to regain that peace of mind which
he had lost.

When Cora received her legacy, and heard that
Percy Lysle had left England, perhaps for ever, without
even a word to her, the sun of her destiny indeed seemed
set in gloom, but she wrestled with her great sorrow,
and none could tell that the brilliant dashing actress, whom
all respected for her virtues and talents, was fighting
with a bruised and lacerated heart. Only to her mother
did Cora confide her sorrow, for never more, she determined, would there be a secret between them, for she
looked upon her conduct to that mother as the cause of
all her troubles.

*   *   *   *   *   *   *

Three years have passed and gone. It is autumn again,
but we look not to the beauties of autumn in England, but
at Nice, on the shore of the deep blue Mediterranean.
The sun is just setting and tinting the waves with its
parting rays, flooding them in a golden light. Almost all
the fashionable world have gone to dinner. One form, however, is still watching the sunset, and it is no other than that
of our heroine, Cora. She looks pale and worn, and has
been advised by the doctors to go to some warm climate

for the winter, and having found that she could afford to retire from the stage for a season, she has come to Nice with her mother. She is still beautiful, but that beauty has a graver, deeper tone. As the lovely girl of twenty she attracted the eye, but as the woman of twenty-three she touches the heart. You see plainly that she has suffered, but that has refined her, and separated the dross from the pure gold. Yes, before her troubles Cora was a loving, faulty, warm-hearted girl, now she is a deep-thinking, pure-minded, high-souled woman. As she sits watching the last golden rays die away, a voice that thrills her soul with a flood of pleasure utters her name. She turns, thinking it must be a dream, but it is real, it is Percy Lysle who stands beside her!

Yes, Percy Lysle! After three long years they have met by chance or destiny by the deep blue waters.

"Still Cora Wilton?" asks Percy, after the first greeting, in a trembling voice, as though he feared to hear the answer, lest it should be a death blow to all his newly formed hopes.

" Yes, still Cora Wilton."

" Thank God ; and now, Cora, I have a sad tale to tell you of weakness and wrong."

And Percy told Cora the history of his life, passing over nothing. "After my cousin's death," he said, "I became a wanderer over the earth, seeking peace, but in vain. Do what I would, I found it impossible to shut out your image from my heart, and fate has brought about this meeting. Say, Cora, can you give me your love, will you be my wife?"

What Cora's answer was we cannot tell, but about six weeks after a quiet marriage was solemnized in a little chapel dedicated to Our Lady (for Percy belonged to the ancient faith), and afterwards in the English church, in which Percy Lysle and Cora played the principal parts.

Our tale is nearly finished, dear reader. Cora having ridden through the storm, although once nearly shipwrecked, is now safe in harbour, and although winds may arise, and waves threaten, she has a protector to help her bear any and every trial.

One more incident and we have finished. Some three days after the marriage of Cora, Nice was thrown into consternation by a frightful suicide, an English gentleman had thrown himself from the top window of his hotel. Although there was no hope of his life, he was not killed on the spot. He was rich, people said, but had no one with him on whose love or attention he could rely. Therefore Percy, at Cora's request, went to see the sufferer; but little did he think to recognise in the broken and bruised mass his bitter enemy Algernon Lance! The wretched man knew Percy at once; he was suffering intense agony, and doubtless judging Percy by himself, thought he had come to gloat over the fall of his enemy; but great was his surprise when Percy told him that he had come to be of use, thinking to find a stranger, but now would remain with him, if he wished it.

"Can you forgive me?" said the dying man.

"Yes," said Percy; "I forgive all."

Algernon Lance was silent for some moments, and then said, as though talking to himself: "Perhaps there is some truth in the old women's tales about an hereafter; but it is too late for me." After this he became delirious, and raved about a figure who continually followed him, and to escape from which he had thrown himself from the window. That night he died. Percy looked for traces of papers to see who his friends were, but in vain. There was a large sum of money and some valuable personal effects, but no clue to his life or family. His death, like his life, was a dark mystery, and saving from the ravings of delirium, no clue could be traced to the cause of his self-destruction. He was buried in a nameless grave, and Percy gave the money and valuables into the hands of the police. So passed away, one who had advantages of youth, beauty, and talents, but who, instead of using them for the glory of Almighty God, had made them the means to lure men on to their destruction. But he had his reward. Verily, "The wages of sin is death."

Mr. Earl, in the society of his children, at last enjoyed

that peace which had been so long a stranger to his heart, and looked forward to the time when his work in this world should be finished, and he should meet those dear ones above who had gone before. Maud was ever fresh in his memory, and her gentle sweetness had imperceptibly led him to think of higher things than the mere tinsel honours of this world. She had been the means of bringing the man nearer to his God, and so sweet Maud had not lived in vain.

THE END.

BILLING, PRINTER, GUILDFORD.

A SEASONABLE GIFT.

THE

ST. JAMES' CHRISTMAS BOX

FOR 1869

Bearing the Royal Arms.
Will be inlaid with Gold,
Handsomely coloured,
Filled with a Story,
By the Author of "George Geith."
Beautifully printed.
Splendidly Illustrated.
Specially adapted for a Christmas Present.
Price One Shilling.
By Post, Fifteen Stamps.
If sent from the Office, carefully wrapped.
Exchanged if damaged.
If an early copy be desired,
Notice the Name, and Order at once
Of any Bookseller,
Anywhere.
Or direct to the Office.
Not forgetting to ask for

THE ST. JAMES' CHRISTMAS BOX FOR 1869,

Which will be Ready November 15th.

LONDON : F. E. ARNOLD,
ST. JAMES' MAGAZINE OFFICE, 49, ESSEX STREET,
STRAND, W.C.